Readers all over the country love
THE SANIBEL SUNSET DETECTIVE

"It's probably one of the best books I've ever read. I kept on wanting to read it because it was such a page-turner. I also love the fact that it's based on Sanibel and Captiva, probably my two favorite places in the world. I am looking forward to the next in the series!"

Evan Magno, Cranston, Rhode Island

"What a hoot it was! I laughed out loud, cried, and never could figure out who was doing what. In other words, I loved it!"

Linda Miller, Sanibel Island, Florida

"Excellent! I can't wait for the next one!"

Peter Digout, St. Peter's, Nova Scotia

"Well, it's 1:41 a.m. and I just turned off my Petzl head-lamp after finishing the book ... damn good read! Took me four hours."

Gordon Burns, Milton, Ontario

"I loved the pace, the humor, the setting, of course, and especially the characters—Tree and Freddie. We're eagerly awaiting the next six Tree and Freddie adventures. Thanks for this one."

he is doing—in work and in life. Despite all the death and mayhem surrounding him, he never forgets what is important to him—the love he shares with his wife and his sense of humor. As he stumbles through his first case, not sure who he can trust, the reader is able to tag along for the ride but unable to predict the outcome. As you turn the pages, you will discover many surprises, yet you will also find something we all need—a smile."

Carl Baker, Virginia, author of To Defend Against All Enemies

"A great read!"

Ries Boers, Milton, Ontario

"I enjoyed The Sanibel Sunset Detective. It often takes me a few paragraphs to get into a book, but I was hooked immediately. I somehow identify with the main character! It was fun reading it. I look forward to the next one."

Carole Grant, Toronto, Ontario

"Yesterday I read the entire book and enjoyed all of it. It was intriguing, interesting, and kept me wanting to read more. Thank you for the entertainment."

Tina Hayes, Walpole, Maine

THE
SANIBEL
SUNSET
DETECTIVE
RETURNS

Also by Ron Base

Fiction

Matinee Idol
Foreign Object
Splendido
Magic Man
The Strange
The Sanibel Sunset Detective

Non-fiction

The Movies of the Eighties (with David Haslam)
If the Other Guy Isn't Jack Nicholson, I've Got the Part
Marquee Guide to Movies on Video
Cuba Portrait of an Island (with Donald Nausbuam)

www.ronbase.com
Read Ron's blog at
www.ronbase.wordpress.com
Contact Ron at
ronbase@ronbase.com

THE SANIBEL
SUNSET
DETECTIVE
RETURNS

a novel

RON BASE

Library and Archives Canada Cataloguing in Publication

Base, Ron, 1948-
The Sanibel Sunset Detective Returns / Ron Base.

ISBN 978-0-9736955-5-7

I. Title.

PS8553.A784S27 2011   C813'.54   C2011-906785-4

West-End Books
80 Front St. East, Suite 605
Toronto, Ontario
Canada M5E 1T4

Cover Design: Bridgit Stone-Budd
Text Design: Ric Base
Electronic formatting: Ric Base

First Edition

For Vallée B

You left too early, old friend.

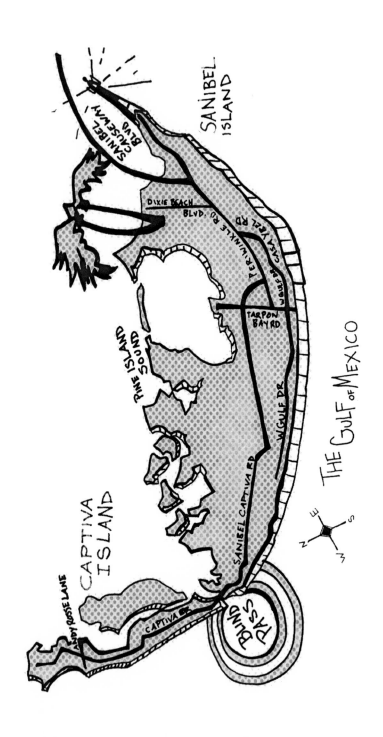

1

"It begins in darkness," Tree Callister said, seated behind his desk on the second floor of the Sanibel-Captiva Chamber of Commerce Visitors Center. "Then a door opens and there is light, and a lone rider appears out of the desert."

"John Wayne as Ethan Edwards," Rex Baxter said. Rex was the president of the Sanibel-Captiva Chamber of Commerce. A former actor in B-pictures, he and Tree had been friends ever since Tree was a reporter in Chicago and appeared on Rex's afternoon movie show on local TV.

Tree said: "*The Searchers* isn't about hate and revenge versus love and forgiveness. It's about death. We come through darkness briefly into light. That door soon closes, and we are in darkness again. Life and death."

"John Wayne didn't like horses," Rex Baxter said.

"What do you mean he didn't like horses?" Todd Jackson, the general manager of Sanibel Biohazard, sounded shocked. "He was John Wayne, for Pete's sake."

"John Wayne didn't like horses," Rex repeated with the patient calm of a man who knows what he is talking about.

"He spent his life sitting on a horse. How could he not like horses?"

"Maybe that's why he didn't like them," Rex said. "I read that somewhere. Drove him crazy, those horses. He preferred his yacht. A converted minesweeper."

"John Wayne on a yacht," Todd said. He sounded deflated. "I don't believe it."

"With the Duke you get a kind of authoritative masculinity totally absent from the screen today," Rex continued. "It's laughed at now. If Duke had doubts or second thoughts, he kept his mouth shut about them. He just wrinkled his brow, looked off into the distance and then saddled up and went out and did what needed to be done. Something kind of reassuring about that."

Todd sipped his coffee and said, "You know about these things, Tree. Did John Wayne like horses?"

"When I was a young reporter at the *Trib*," Tree said, "they sent me to interview Wayne at his home in Newport Beach, California."

Rex looked at him. "I didn't know that."

"This was before I knew you. You're right about the horses. He looked much more like a successful Republican businessman than he did the quintessential cowboy star. He made me drink a lot of tequila. Then he took me out onto a terrace that overlooked the water. Across the bay was an old-fashioned pavilion. The Duke said he used to go dancing over there as a kid. He threw his arm around me and said, 'These days, the only two things lit up around here at night are that pavilion—and the old Duke!'"

Everyone laughed. Rex slapped his knees and said, "Well, John Wayne is long gone and the world is a different place. The Duke was lucky. He only had to kiss girls, ride horses, and shoot people. I have to worry about the annual Kiwanis spaghetti dinner."

"Yeah, I should get to the office," Todd said. "I've got a job over in Lehigh Acres. Elderly woman died in her apartment. No one found her for a week."

"Sad," Rex said. "You run out of options. There comes a day and no matter what, you just can't get through. The door closes. It's permanent darkness. Even John Wayne couldn't avoid it. Then what?"

"Then you call me in, and I clean up the mess," Todd said.

A white-haired man appeared in the doorway. Ray Dayton, owner of Dayton's supermarket, focused his laser-like gaze on Rex and said, "I thought we were picking up the spaghetti sauce this morning."

Tree's wife, Freddie, worked for Ray at Dayton's. Tree and Ray did not get along. Ray thought Tree was a loser who did not deserve to be married to Freddie. Tree thought Ray was a pompous, self-important fool who happened to be rich and employ his wife.

"And good morning to you, too, Ray," Rex said. He looked at his watch. "Sorry. The time got away from me." He pointed a finger at Tree. "You're volunteering to help us out with the Kiwanis spaghetti dinner."

"I am?" Tree said.

"We need another salad guy," Todd said. "I just hope you're up to the challenge."

Tree looked at Ray. "Better make sure it's all right with Ray."

Ray shifted his tight jaw around and studied a point somewhere above Tree's head. "We can use all the help we can get," he mumbled.

Rex rose to his feet. "Okay, it's done. Tree, you're officially volunteering for salad duty. Ray, let's go get that sauce. I think we're going to have our biggest year ever."

"You say that every year," Todd said.

Ray abruptly turned and headed down the stairs. Rex and Todd traded glances.

"Don't know what's wrong with him lately," Rex said.

"He's a jerk," Todd pronounced. "A character defect Ray's had to live with his entire life."

"Or maybe home trouble," Rex said.

"You speak from experience?" Todd said.

"Lots of experience. Too much experience." Rex started for the door. "Come on, Todd. Let's get out of here so Tree can get to work and pay the high rent I charge him every month."

"Yeah, the clients are lined up out the door," Todd said.

"Those are called tourists," Rex said.

Rex and Todd left Tree alone in his office. He swiveled around in his chair, drank more of the Starbucks coffee Rex brought each morning, and stared out the window, contemplating the state of his life. Although he had recently been in the news, saving a twelve-year-old boy from the clutches of a gang of body parts dealers, the notoriety had so far failed to attract new clients to the Sanibel Sunset Detective Agency.

Tree had started the agency after arriving on the island with his wife, the remarkable Fredryka Stayner, known to all as Freddie. Tired of the grind of big city corporate life with a large supermarket chain, Freddie, on a wild whim, had taken a job running Dayton's for Ray Dayton.

Tree had just turned sixty, and even though he had come to Sanibel often as a child, he felt very much the outsider here, robbed of his lifelong identity as a Chicago newspaper reporter, cast into a wondrous but strange world; an old world really, lost and found on these barrier islands, a world without strip malls or theme parks or fast food, where what was once natural and true about Florida survived still.

He had arrived in this world and loved it, but beneath its bright sun he existed in darkness and confusion, feeling adrift in paradise.

Thus, the Sanibel Sunset Detective was born amid derisive snickers and much head shaking. He couldn't really blame anyone for the way they reacted. After all, what did he know about being a detective? And who needed a detective on Sanibel Island, not exactly America's crime capital?

No one apparently. At least not lately.

Thus W. Tremain Callister, Esq.—Tree—had time to think about John Wayne and that night at Newport Beach. How vivid it still seemed, and yet how far away it was, another time, featuring a young man long gone and a movie icon so much a part of celluloid legend it seemed hard to imagine he was ever a living, breathing human being.

Tree could barely remember anything about his children or wife from that time, and yet he clearly recalled every detail of his encounter with John Wayne. Crazy. Ridiculous. Unfair to children and former wives. After all, the children and even the ex-wives remained; the movie icons faded.

Tree heard something and looked up to see a big woman fill the doorway. He hadn't heard her come up the stairs, although given the size of her, it was surprising he hadn't.

As she stood there, the woman seemed at a loss for words, as though in looking at Tree she had seen something she had not expected to see.

"Hi," Tree said. "What can I do for you?"

That appeared to shake the woman out of her reverie.

"I'm looking for help," she said.

"Yes?"

"Could you give me directions?"

Tree regarded her with a quizzical expression. "They can help you downstairs."

The woman lumbered into the room. "I'm lost," she said. "Lost in your eyes."

For a moment, his visitor's rugged face remained solemn. Then it broke into a crooked grin. "I'm kidding you," she said.

She was three inches taller than Tree, which made her about six feet, four inches, and weighing in at over two hundred pounds. The bright aqua-colored pantsuit would make her visible for miles. Short-cropped coppery hair framed a tough, masculine face, its surface as pitted and scarred as a moonscape. She reminded Tree of the French actor Jean Gabin; Jean in drag.

"Sit down, miss—"

"Clowers," she said. "Ms. Ferne Clowers." Her voice was a deep growl, the result of many years spent filling her throat with cigarette smoke. She settled into the chair, shifting around broad shoulders. "You're Tree Callister?"

"That's right," he said.

"One of the Sanibel Sunset detectives?"

"I'm *the* Sanibel Sunset Detective," he said.

That unleashed a smile that would send small children screaming in terror.

"Exactly," she said. "That's what I need, someone who can take care of himself."

Could Tree Callister take care of himself? Most days he doubted it, but Ferne Clowers didn't need to know that.

"I read about you in the papers." The craggy smile shrank into something smaller and more secretive and surprisingly feminine. "Someone shot you."

"Yes," Tree said.

"A man of action," she said.

That was the problem with being shot in South Florida. Everyone assumed that denoted some sort of tough guy persona. As far as he could ascertain, having survived the experience, it merely confirmed that he could stop a bullet, which did not require much in the way of toughness. It involved no more than being in the way of the bullet.

"I've got to meet someone," Ferne Clowers said.

"Okay," Tree said.

"I don't want to meet this person alone. That's where you come in, see? I want to hire you to come along with me."

"To accompany you to this meeting?"

"Won't take long. The afternoon, maybe"

"Where?"

"Matlacha."

"On Pine Island."

"Take us about forty minutes."

"Why don't you want to meet this person alone?"

"What difference does it make?"

Tree said, "I have a simple rule of thumb, Ms. Clowers. Never walk into a situation without knowing how to walk out again."

Which wasn't quite true. Tree recently had walked into a number of situations he had no idea how to get out of, accounting, perhaps, for how he got shot. Yet even he, dumb as he was about these things, required more information than Ferne Clowers so far was willing to provide.

"You'll walk out all right," she said. "Slippery's harmless enough, I suppose."

"Slippery?"

"Bailey Street. Everyone calls him Slippery."

"Slippery Street?"

She did not appear to recognize the irony. "He owes me money," she said. "I sold him a boat last month and he's been making trouble about it ever since. Finally, he's agreed to pay. But like I say, I don't want to go there alone.

I'm a woman after all. Anything can happen. I need a man of action at my side."

"I don't know how much of a man of action I'm going to be for you," Tree said.

Ferne said, "You'll have to do. What sort of rates do you charge?"

"Two hundred dollars a day, plus expenses," Tree said.

"Here's what I propose," Ferne Clowers said. "I will pay you five hundred dollars in cash. Two hundred and fifty dollars now. The rest as soon as we're finished with Slippery. That's not bad money for an afternoon's work."

"When do you want to do this?"

"Now. This afternoon," Ferne said. As though he should have known.

She opened her handbag, reached in, withdrew a wad of cash and proceeded to place two one hundred dollar bills on his desk. They were followed by two twenties and a ten.

Tree put on his reading glasses for a better view of the money. "That's not much notice," he said.

"I'm interrupting a very busy day, I'm sure." Not too sarcastic, accompanied by a disarming smile.

Tree removed his glasses and scooped up the bills, dropping them into the top desk drawer. Ferne announced they would drive out to Matlacha in her car. She would drop him back at the chamber as soon as they finished. This was reasonable, Tree decided, since Ferne would never fit comfortably into his Volkswagen Beetle.

"Okay," Tree said. "Let's get going."

Ferne was on her feet storming out the door. In the outer office, one of the chamber's volunteers gave a start as Ferne breezed down the stairs. Tree locked the office before following. As he descended the stairs, he saw the volunteer shaking his head.

Outside, Ferne charged around the corner of the Visitors Center to where she had parked her car, a dazzling 1985 convertible Cadillac Biarritz Eldorado, black, with a cherry-red leather interior bright enough to make Tree squint.

"You don't see a whole lot of these around," Tree said.

"One in a million, like me," Ferne said. "Hop in. I'll take you for a ride."

Tree said he hoped she was kidding. She just grinned as she gunned it out of the parking lot. She flipped the radio on. George Thorogood howled "Bad to the Bone."

"Love that mother," she announced over the music. "Time for a little Jimbo. Kick the glove compartment open, will you, Tree?"

He popped the lid and out dropped a half empty bottle of Jim Beam bourbon. She grabbed it out of his hands, propped it between her legs, and deftly twisted off the cap. "Join me."

"I don't know whether you are aware of this, Ferne. But you're not supposed to drink while you drive."

"You're kidding," she said, taking a deep swig. "Boy, they really are trying to take our rights and freedoms away, aren't they? I mean what kind of country is it, a woman can't have a drink?"

She took another swig.

2

The tops of Cape Coral bungalows whisked by on either side of the flat strip of Veterans Memorial Parkway as George Thorogood sang "Who Do You Love."

Ferne settled back against the red leather, one hand on the wheel, an arm on the open window. Tree had convinced her to put "Jimbo" back in the glove compartment.

Slapping the flat of her big hand against the outside of the car in time to the music, Ferne made a left on SW Pine Island Road and then drove toward Pine Island.

A series of blue and green and yellow match boxes appeared along either side of the highway—the art galleries and restaurants of Matlacha, evidence of a more unconventional, therefore more interesting, Florida that somehow survived in a world of strip malls and fast food franchises.

Ferne turned onto a gravel drive next to a yellow and blue rowboat mounted on a pedestal of rocks. Someone had painted "Shipwrecked in Matlacha" in black letters along the boat's bow.

Tree got out of the Cadillac and stretched his legs. Ferne was already out, buzzing past a souvenir shop, its walls lined with brightly-colored sharks, sea horses, and star fish. For one fearful instant, Tree thought she would plough into a line of rainbow-colored ceramic pots set on the ground. At the last moment, she veered away, turned, and flashed one of those transformative smiles that momentarily made her seem like someone else entirely; the giant-size girlfriend on a date.

"You okay there, Tree?"

"We're on our way to find your friend, right?"

"Well, I wouldn't call Slippery a friend, exactly," Ferne amended. "Maybe after I get my money back. Right now, he's just a difficult son of a bitch."

She disappeared around the corner. He hurried after her and found her approaching a white shrimp boat tied to a dock. The *Busted Flush* was small and compact, outfitted with line pullers, trap haulers and three wing nets hung from the masts.

Ferne clomped onto the dock, causing the pelicans nestled there, their long pouched beaks folded against their chests, to jump in alarm and quickly fly away. Ignoring the disturbed birds, Ferne thudded to a stop beside the boat. She leaned forward, cupping her hand around her mouth, hollering, "Slippery? You there?"

There was no response. Tree came onto the dock and stood behind Ferne, uncertain exactly what role he was supposed to play. A couple of the pelicans, having retreated to the dock's edge, eyed the interlopers with what looked to Tree like a great deal of suspicion.

Finally, a voice from the boat hollered back: "That you, Ferne?"

"It's me, Slippery."

"Who's that with you?"

"Friend," said Ferne.

"Come on board," the boat voice said.

Ferne wobbled uncertainly. Tree stepped forward to take her hand. She shook him away. "Get aboard first, Tree, and then help me down."

A breeze came up suddenly, sweeping across the water, causing the *Busted Flush* to sway and tilt, pulling against its moorings. Tree jumped down onto the moving deck, and almost lost his balance. He righted himself and then turned and reached his hand up to her. She did not move. Her face had gone blank. "It's too choppy," she said in a croaked voice. "Make sure Slippery's alone."

"What?"

"Slippery. Make sure he's alone."

Tree turned toward the tiny windowed cabin. Another gust of wind sent the boat against the dock again, harder this time. Tree braced his legs on the deck. Through the glass's reflection, he could make out movement.

"Hey," Tree said.

A shape moved forward and Slippery Street stepped out of the cabin. Unshaven, his thinning hair in disarray, he wore a pair of cargo shorts. Leathery skin stretched across a skeletal torso. He held a gun in his hand.

Tree, fighting to keep his balance on the deck, looked at the gun as Slippery pointed it at him.

Slippery pulled the trigger.

3

The gun did not go off.

Another wind gust caused the boat to rock some more. Slippery Street braced himself against the bulkhead and pulled the trigger a second time. Nothing happened again. Tree stood there, frozen with fear, realizing that somehow Ferne had clambered onto the boat and now stood beside him. He cried out, "Ferne," in a high, panicky voice. She kept her eyes fixed on the gun quivering in Slippery's boney hand.

Slippery snarled an expletive, and then reached down, fumbling with something around his ankle. The next thing he had a straight razor in his hand, its long blade gleaming.

Ferne Clowers said, "Slippery, don't."

To Tree's amazement—not to mention Slippery's—Ferne slapped the razor away. It clattered to the deck. Slippery gave Ferne a look of absolute astonishment. "What the hell are you doing?"

Ferne said, "I can't do this. I'm sorry, I can't." She turned to Tree: "Run. Get out of here."

"Dammit to hell," Slippery said.

Tree stumbled off the *Busted Flush* onto the dock, scattering the pelicans. He glanced back at Ferne and her pal Slippery still standing stock still on the boat deck as if they had turned to pillars of salt.

Tree picked up speed, expecting to hear the telltale pop of a gunshot, confirmation Slippery had finally got his gun working.

But there was only his increasingly labored breathing until he regained the street. The everyday sounds of a normal world resumed; the world wherein most people were not trying to shoot one another. He found himself among tourist throngs intent on shopping or deciding on a restaurant for lunch. A rotund woman with short gray hair looked at him and said, "Are you all right?"—evidence that he did not look at all right.

Winded, Tree came finally to a stop. He heard a sound behind him and swung around in time to see the Cadillac Eldorado roar onto the highway, headed toward Cape Coral. He caught a glimpse of Ferne hunched behind the wheel. She was staring straight ahead.

Slippery huddled beside her.

4

Tree told sheriff's deputies at Matlacha that someone had tried to shoot him.

They appeared skeptical since there had been no gunshots and no witnesses. They dutifully took down the particulars of what had happened, but they seemed much more impressed by Freddie when she arrived at the police station wearing Dolce and Gabbana.

The deputies were not anxious to do much more than steal glances at Freddie and toss the case to the Sanibel Island police where, as far as they were concerned, the incident originated and thus more properly should be handled.

Freddie drove Tree back to Sanibel in her red Mercedes. She did not sound much more convinced than the Matlacha deputies.

"Let me get this straight," she said. "A woman hired you, brought you out here, and then tried to kill you."

"Except that after the gun went off, or more to the point, did not go off, Ferne had a change of heart and when this guy Slippery pulled a straight razor, she knocked it out of his hand and probably saved my life."

"And you don't have any idea who she is or why she would want to kill you?"

"I've never seen this woman before in my life."

"You sound like Bill Clinton.

"Do I?"

"You could be dead right now."

"Would you miss me?"

"For a couple of hours at least." She reached over and touched his knee, a reassuring gesture. "Seriously, though. We should take this seriously."

"I know that. I am taking it seriously."

"How are you feeling?"

"I think I'm okay," he lied.

"I was hoping you would say something like, 'but determined to find a job that doesn't get me killed.'"

"And what job would that be?"

"It's just that I can't help wondering how well suited you are to this kind of work."

"If it's any consolation, I wonder myself."

"Yet you keep on, my love."

"Am I crazy or what?"

"Stubborn may have something to do with it."

"Or stupid," Tree added.

Freddie did not argue the point.

———

At the Sanibel Island police station, Tree was placed in the same conference room he occupied the last time he was there.

He sat at the table, drumming his fingers, waiting, trying not to look nervous, feeling naked and exposed under the watchful eye of the video camera he knew was installed in here. In rooms like this, you always felt more like the perpetrator than the victim.

The conference room door opened and Cee Jay Boone stepped inside. The last time Tree saw her, Cee Jay and her partner, Mel Scott, had tried to kill him.

Attempted murder and forcible confinement charges had been dropped when Cee Jay agreed to testify against Scott. Then everything got thrown out on a technicality. Scott pleaded guilty to assault and was serving a three-year prison sentence. Meanwhile, the Sanibel Police had no choice but to lift Cee Jay's suspension and allow her back to work, pending the outcome of a department review.

"How are you doing, Tree?" she said, closing the door.

Cee Jay had allowed her hair to fill out, and the ten pounds she had gained strained her midnight blue pantsuit.

"I'm doing okay under the circumstances," he said. "How about you, Cee Jay?"

Under the circumstances, I guess you could say I'm doing okay, too. But imagine my concern when I heard what happened to you at Matlacha."

Cee Jay did not sound at all concerned. She seated herself across from Tree and flipped open a notebook.

"Excuse me, Cee Jay, but given our history together, should you and I even be talking?"

"I suppose you've got a point, Tree. In a better world they would have assigned another detective to this. However, it is not a better world, there is a staff shortage, and so here I am."

"Yes, here you are," Tree said unhappily.

Cee Jay smiled and said, "You say someone tried to kill you?"

"That's right."

"Seems like someone's always trying to kill you, Tree."

"You should know, Cee Jay."

She ignored that reference to their troubled past and said, "Who is trying to kill you this time?"

"A skinny, unshaven little runt named Slippery Street."

Cee Jay's expression remained neutral.

"That's what Ferne said his name was."

Cee Jay looked down at the papers she had brought in with her; a report from the Malacha sheriff's department, perhaps. "Ferne would be this Ferne Clowers. The woman who supposedly hired you to accompany her to Matlacha."

"That's right," Tree said. "She came to my office this morning."

"And you had never seen this woman before?"

"Correct."

"Yet you say this unknown woman conspired with a skinny guy to kill you."

"A skinny, unshaven guy."

"Maybe you shouldn't be so surprised that people want to kill you, Tree." Cee Jay adopted a deadpan look that was hard to read—or maybe not so hard at all.

The door opened, and a tall, lanky man entered wearing a beige suit. Brown hair shot through with gold highlights was swept back from a high, sunburned forehead. "Sorry I'm late," the man said. "Did I miss anything?"

"Tree, this is my new partner, Detective Owen Markfield. Owen, this is Tree Callister, the private detective I was telling you about."

Owen Markfield flopped into a chair. He did not offer to shake hands.

He said, "The cheap detective. Isn't that what they call you, Callister? The cheap detective? You work for seven dollars, something like that?"

His opening sentence defined him: Owen Markfield would not be playing the good cop.

"I've gotten more expensive," Tree said.

"Tree was just telling me how someone he'd never met before tried to kill him up at Matlacha this afternoon."

Owen Markfield focused startling blue eyes. He had a square jaw with a dimple in the center, like a young Kirk Douglas.

"Go ahead Tree, tell us what happened." Cee Jay made it sound as though she was asking him to lie through his teeth.

As quickly as he could, Tree recounted the morning's events, beginning with Ferne's unexpected appearance at his office. Owen Markfield made a face as Tree finished. "The gun misfired?"

"It didn't go off," Tree said.

"What kind of gun was it?"

"I don't know. A black gun. A gun that didn't shoot me. I don't know a lot about guns."

Markfield looked surprised. "You don't have a gun?"

"No."

"You're a private detective, and you don't have a gun."

"That's right," Tree said.

"The gunless detective," Markfield said.

Cee Jay again consulted the pages before her. "Ferne Clowers? You're certain that's the woman's name?"

"That's the name she gave me."

"There's no Ferne Clowers in the police data base."

"What does that mean?"

"For one thing, it means no one named Ferne Clowers has a criminal record."

"What about Bailey Street?"

"You mean Slippery Street?"

"She said his real name is Bailey Street."

Cee Jay sat back, shaking her head. "Nothing shows up on him, either."

Markfield pointed a slim, accusatory finger. "Two complete strangers. A woman the size of a house. A skinny guy."

"A skinny, unshaven guy."

"The woman pretends to hire you. Lures you up to Matlacha where she has an accomplice waiting with a gun that doesn't go off."

"Don't forget the razor."

"Okay, the razor. He comes at you with a razor. The woman knocks the razor out of his hand and tells you to get the hell out of there."

"That's what happened," Tree said.

"I talked to the sheriff's department up there a few minutes ago. No one saw a black Cadillac Eldorado driven by a big woman and a little guy named Slippery. No one saw anything—and you didn't get a license number for the car?"

"No," Tree said.

"You're a detective, Tree," Markfield said. "Detectives get license numbers."

Tree said, "What about the shrimp boat?"

"The *Busted Flush* is owned by a Mr. McDonald who lives in Fort Lauderdale," Cee Jay replied. "He leases the boat to local fishermen. He doesn't know anyone named Ferne Clowers or Slippery Street. As far as he knows the boat has been sitting at dockside in Matlacha for the past week."

"So what are you saying? I'm lying to you? I made this all up?"

Detectives Cee Jay Boone and Owen Markfield just looked at him. No one said anything.

————

Freddie was waiting for him at the bottom of the ramp leading to the police station. "How did it go?"

"They didn't believe a word I said."

"Let's go to the car," Freddie said. "I'll drive you back to the Visitors Center."

Tree followed her to the Mercedes. "This is the part where you're supposed to say, 'Darling, even though they don't believe you, I do.'"

"Darling, even though they don't believe you, I do."

"It would help if you could say it as though you mean it."

His cell phone rang. When he opened it up, a familiar voice said, "Good evening, Mr. Callister."

5

Tree crossed McGregor Boulevard to where those legends of American ingenuity, Henry Ford and Thomas Edison, had purchased adjacent summer houses overlooking the Caloosahatchee River. Edison called his place the Seminole Lodge. Ford christened his, the Mangoes. Edison had bought his home first and then convinced his pal Henry to buy the house next door for twenty thousand dollars.

It didn't strike Tree that Ford was exactly throwing his money around.

He walked across the lush grounds to the gray, wood-frame Edison house and went up onto the wide porch with its hanging wicker seats. He watched the crowd around the entrance to Thomas and Mina's bedroom. Two single beds were pushed together, flanked by wicker armchairs with pink cushions that seemed more like Mina than Thomas. He wondered how he would feel about strangers with cameras peering into the Tree and Freddie bedroom in a hundred years or so. He probably did not have to worry about it.

"Edison was hard of hearing, maybe that's why they got along."

Elizabeth Traven glided across the veranda, shimmering in white, silky hair floating to her shoulders, those opaque, fathomless eyes hidden behind dark glasses.

"Otherwise, they were certainly an odd couple. Edison, half deaf, with bad breath and dandruff. Ford, a farmer's son, anti-Semite, anti-union. Hitler loved him."

"You're kidding? Hitler loved Henry Ford?"

"He's the only American mentioned in *Mein Kampf*. Hitler thought Ford the embodiment of what all Germans should become. The Nazis gave him a medal."

Elizabeth was the wife of the disgraced media mogul, Brand Traven. Several months earlier, while her husband languished in prison convicted of obstruction of justice in connection with his collapsed newspaper empire, Elizabeth had hired Tree. She wanted a woman followed, she'd said.

There turned out to be a lot more to it—Elizabeth had become mixed up with a gang of body parts thieves in her desperation to save the life of Traven's thirteen-year-old niece. By the time it was over, Tree had nearly got himself killed.

That's why Freddie urged him not to have anything more to do with Elizabeth Traven. But Tree could not resist. Brand Traven weeks ago had been released from prison after three years, the charges against him thrown out on appeal. Why would Elizabeth want to meet him here? And what could she possibly want to talk to him about?

There was only one way to find out.

Elizabeth looked at two rocking chairs positioned by the railing. "Can you imagine Edison and Ford sitting together out here? I wonder what they talked about."

"How difficult it is to get good help?"

"They were certainly close," Elizabeth said. "When Edison died, Ford insisted his son catch his last breath in a test tube."

"Why would he do that?"

"Who knows? But the test tube still exists. It's in the Henry Ford museum."

"You seem to know a lot about this," Tree said.

"At one point, I considered doing a biography of Ford, but I could never get past the anti-Jewish stuff. He recanted his views, eventually, but it was a case of too little too late."

Before Elizabeth became Traven's wife, she had been a respected journalist and biographer. Despite all the troubles surrounding her husband's imprisonment, she had recently managed to publish a well-received biography of Trotsky.

She removed her sunglasses. The gesture solved few mysteries. Those opaque eyes remained unreadable as she inspected him.

"It's been a while, Mr. Callister. How have you been? Are you fully recovered?"

"From my gunshot wound or my last encounter with you?"

She gave him a tight smile and looked around. "Have you been here before?"

"Not for years," he said.

"Why don't we go over to the Ford house?" she said. "See how the other half lived."

He followed her off the porch. Tourists glanced at her appreciatively. She was out of place among the shorts and the baseball caps and the digital cameras. It was as though she had made a wrong turn on New York's Fifth Avenue and somehow ended up at the Edison Ford Museum.

"So what are you thinking?" As if she knew exactly what he was thinking. He wasn't about to give her that, though, so he fibbed:

"I'm thinking that with all the money these two geezers had, they didn't spend it here. I suppose they used these houses to convince themselves they were just like anyone else."

"You don't like the rich, do you, Mr. Callister?"

"Only rich people like the rich. The rest of us come to peer in their windows and wonder why they spent so much money, or in the case of Edison and Ford, to speculate why they didn't spend more."

"I've decided I don't like the rich, either," she said. "I don't like the way they treat you when you are no longer one of them."

"You're no longer rich, Mrs. Traven?"

She smiled broadly. "I'm just a poor working writer, doing what's necessary to survive."

"And what is necessary to survive?"

"Doing things one never imagines oneself doing. Well, you know all about that, don't you, Mr. Callister?"

"Yes," he said. "I suppose I do."

"Which is why I called you."

"Don't tell me you want to hire me."

"Why is that so surprising?"

"The last time, you employed me to do one thing but in fact you wanted something else entirely."

"Which is to say, what?"

"I don't trust you? Could that be it?"

To demonstrate her honesty, Elizabeth removed her sunglasses a second time. "I suppose I can hardly blame you, can I?"

She kept her gaze trained on him. Those eyes could bore right through him still—and shine with the sincerity of Henry Ford's denials of anti-Semitism.

"It's my husband," she said. "You know he's out of jail?"

"So I've heard."

"It's not an easy time for us, as you can imagine," she continued. "But with Brand's release, the charge against him thrown out, the two of us together again, I thought things might be different."

"But they aren't?"

"The marriage was under considerable strain before the trouble started. I held on, though, stuck it out with him so he didn't have to go through this alone. Even when I had reservations about what it would take to get his niece a liver, I went along. As you know it almost finished me, and you, too, for that matter. But again, I stayed with him, went along with what he wanted."

She replaced the sunglasses, as though she'd had enough honesty for one day.

"I'm no longer willing to put up with his lies and deceit."

"What does that mean, Mrs. Traven?"

"What do a man's lies and deceit usually mean?"

"He's having an affair?"

"I believe that to be the case," she said formally, as though rehearsing the eventual deposition in the matter.

Tree didn't bother to hide his surprise. "Has he been out of prison long enough?"

"How much time do you think men need? My experience is they don't need much time at all. The point is I want you to find out what he's up to."

"You want me to follow Brand Traven?"

"I want you to do whatever is necessary."

"What does he say about this affair?"

"He says nothing. I don't ask him."

"Don't you think you should try talking to him first?"

"Two hundred dollars a day, is that what you still charge?"

"I haven't said I'll take the case," Tree said.

Elizabeth Traven gave a brittle laugh. "You'll take it, Mr. Callister."

"How do you know?"

"Because even after being chased around and shot, and shooting someone yourself, no one takes you any more seriously than they did before. No one wants to hire you. You'll do what I want, all right. You'll do it."

They had stopped near one of the towering orchid-filled mango trees in Mina Edison's opulent gardens. Tree was determined to tell Elizabeth that he could not be bought, that people did take him seriously. He had plenty of clients. Clients coming out of his ears.

He was going to tell her all those things.

She withdrew a thick envelope from her purse and handed it to him. "There's enough in there to keep you going for a couple of weeks."

"I wonder, Mrs. Traven, if the day will come when middle-aged tourists will look at where you lived on Captiva Drive and speculate as to what you were really like. I wonder what they will say. What they will think."

"You keep wondering, Mr. Callister. Meanwhile, I'll get on with things. Because that's what one does. One does not whine or cry. One does what's necessary. One gets on."

She pushed the envelope into his hands. "I want daily reports. I presume you can get started immediately."

He held the envelope as though it was a great weight. But he did not give it back. Apparently satisfied, Elizabeth wheeled and started away, the click of high heels marking her progress along the walkway. He stood with the envelope full of money in his hand, watching as she disappeared among streams of tourists.

And then he saw something else.

A figure darted through the crowd. The same scrawny frame. The same two-day growth of beard.

Slippery Street.

He wore shorts, a gray T-shirt and a baseball cap pulled down over his eyes. He wasn't pointing a gun at Tree. But it had to be Slippery.

Tree brushed past baby boomers inspecting the lives of the rich and the dead. He thought he spotted Slippery by the Edison pool house and ran toward it. He stopped to catch his breath. Someone said, "Edison built the pool in 1910. It was one of the first swimming pools in Florida."

There was no sign of Slippery.

6

Two identical Dodge Durangos were parked in the drive beside their tiny house on Andy Rosse Lane so that Tree had to park the Beetle on the street.

Tree got out and inspected the vehicles. One Dodge was black, the other was red. Tourists tended to park anywhere they could find an empty space, even if it was someone's private driveway. One of the hazards of living on Captiva: there was not a whole lot of parking in paradise.

Tree went inside. Freddie was sitting in the living room with his son Chris and Chris's wife, Kendra. Kendra was a model from Missouri who had been chosen Playmate of the Month for the March 2007 issue of *Playboy* magazine.

Chris and Kendra had met when he was assistant manager at Chicago's legendary Smith and Woolinsky Steak House. They married in 2009 and then started up an online dating service. Tree didn't know what to make of his son being married to someone whom hundreds of thousands of readers had seen naked. He also didn't know what to make of a son leaving the restaurant industry where he had been very successful for what seemed the much more nebulous business of online dating.

Tree said, "This is a surprise."

Chris's smile was frozen in place. "Here we are, Dad." Chris stood and awkwardly embraced his father.

He was tall and slim, a younger version of his mother, Judy. She had been the first of too many Tree Callister marriages; the dutiful young housewife who only wanted a family and a partner who came home at night. Tree in those days was not that man. The marriage had failed miserably. His fault; all of it.

None of his three children resembled him. Just as well. Was this a message? You're a lousy parent. This is your punishment: none of your kids will look like you.

Chris did have one thing in common with his father: eyeglasses. They gave him a vaguely professorial air; an air totally misplaced since Christopher had scant interest in anything intellectual. His hair was light brown and close-cropped—the style of young people these days, Tree mused. His parents would have been delighted. Growing up in the sixties this was the style they demanded of their kids' hair. Naturally, the kids wanted it long, much to the older generation's unending horror. Now the children of the long-haired kids favored short hair.

The gods must be laughing.

Chris let go of his father. That uneasy smile was still pasted to his face like something he couldn't shake off. Tree coughed and adjusted his glasses. Kendra rose languidly. Kendra did everything languidly, Tree noted. She was small and blond with a button nose you could not pay for and dazzling blue eyes to die for. The Playmate in flower.

She embraced Tree, and that did not seem nearly so awkward. "Papa Tree," she said. When had she decided to call him that? He couldn't remember. It was sweet and endearing—and totally irritating. Papa Tree? It was not so long ago that he dated women who looked like Kendra. Well, okay, maybe it was a while ago.

He managed a grin and said, "How was the drive?"

"Long and boring," Kendra said, flopping back down on the sofa and stretching tanned legs.

"Maybe you should have driven down together," Tree said.

"Then I'd have to listen to your son playing that rap crap."

Tree looked at Christopher. "You like rap?"

He said, a tad defensively, "What's wrong with rap?"

"I like Papa Tree music," Kendra said, throwing Tree a smile. How did Kendra get her teeth so white? He felt his face redden. What was *that* all about?

"What's Papa Tree music?"

"The Beatles," Chris said.

"Some Beach Boys, too," Kendra said. "Maybe a little Procol Harum."

Tree didn't like Procol Harum but decided not to say anything.

"Is anyone hungry?" Freddie said. "It's late but I can throw something together."

"That would be great, Freddie," Chris said. "I keep telling Kendra you're the best cook in Florida."

"That's because I am most definitely *not* the best cook in Chicago," Kendra said.

Tree could not imagine Kendra at a stove.

"Has anyone offered drinks?" Tree said.

"I was just about to do that," Freddie said. "How about some wine?"

"You don't have anything stronger, Dad? Scotch?"

"You drink scotch?"

"Kendra likes to have a glass, too." As if Kendra's fondness for scotch explained everything.

"I can go to the corner and get a bottle," Tree said.

"I'll go with you," Chris said.

"I'll get dinner started," Freddie said. She looked at Kendra. "What about it, Kendra? Do you feel like giving me a hand?"

"Sure." Kendra sounded unenthusiastic.

They walked over to the Island Store. The tourists were gone for the night. A layer of humidity had settled, bringing a stillness that had the effect of drawing Tree closer to his son. At least he thought it did. Chris raised his arms above his head, taking deep breaths, as if to shake off the tension he was feeling. "Nice to be here," he said.

"Good to have you—even if it is unexpected."

"Chris and Kendra, always up for a little of the unexpected."

"Everything okay?"

"Sure thing there, Papa Tree," Chris said with a smirk. "How's the private detective business?"

"Quiet," Tree said. He thought of Ferne Clowers and Slippery Street and the gun that misfired. Well, maybe not so quiet. But his son didn't need to know that, at least not now.

"So you're still doing that?"

"You sound surprised."

"You know, after what happened."

"What happened?"

"You getting shot and everything. That didn't put you off?"

"Hey, what's getting shot every once in a while," Tree said.

"My father, man of action," Chris said. He did not sound impressed.

Chris didn't know the half of it. Tree said, "Not that much action."

Chris chuckled. "More than I would have imagined."

They reached the Island Store and went inside. Chris picked up two bottles of single malt scotch. He paid and they went outside again and started back for the house. Chris became tenser. He took another deep breath.

"Listen, Dad," he said. "We may be staying for a while."

"Okay," Tree said.

"We just had to get away from Chicago, that's all. Clear the air a bit."

"What about your online dating business?"

"That's on hold for the time being."

"You're sure everything is all right?"

"No, it's not, frankly." Chris stopped and looked at his father. "We've run into a bit of a rough patch lately. We need a place where we can just hang out so we can have a little peace and quiet and figure our next move."

"Anything I can do to help?"

"In your role as father or private detective?" Edged with sarcasm.

Tree ignored it. "You're welcome to stay as long as you like. Do you need money?"

Chris grinned. "That would be the role of the father. Thanks, but all we need right now is some hospitality."

"You've always got that, Chris."

"What about Freddie?"

"What about her?"

"Will she be all right with this?"

"She'll be fine," Tree said. "Is everything all right between you and Kendra?"

Chris ducked the question by saying, "Also, I'd appreciate it if you didn't say anything about the two of us being here."

"Okay," Tree said, not sure how he was going to keep that quiet in the small world that constituted life on the island.

"You know, it's no one's business what we're up to, and right now we just want to keep a low profile."

"Sure," Tree said.

That night Chris drank too much scotch. He played with the chicken Freddie had prepared without eating it. Kendra had a couple of glasses of white wine, and kept her wits about her. If she was worried, it didn't show. At ten o'clock she hauled Chris off to bed. Tree and Freddie retreated to the kitchen to clean up. Tree told her about his conversation with Chris.

"So what do you make of that?" she asked him.

"I don't know, but I suspect their business is in trouble. I'll find out more. In the meantime, though, we have house guests for the next little while. Are you okay with that?"

"She has a tramp stamp, you know."

"A tramp stamp? What's that?"

"A tattoo on her lower back. In her case, it's a blood-red rose. You've seen it."

"I have not," Tree protested. "What's more, I've never heard of a tramp stamp. And you didn't answer my question."

"I'm fine," Freddie said. "I must say you do a masterful job of at least trying to keep your eyes off her."

"You think I can't keep my eyes off Kendra?"

"I doubt the man exists who can. That's her blessing and her curse, isn't it?"

"Is it?"

"The great thing is, everyone wants her. The awful thing is, everyone wants her. Creates a lot of tension and confusion, I suspect."

"I don't want her," Tree said.

"I know you wouldn't actually sleep with her or anything," Freddie said. "But she is the stuff of male fantasy. It won't last much longer, but it is there right now, and boy, it's something to behold."

"I'm not sure what you're getting at," Tree said.

"I just wonder if that doesn't cause trouble for them, that's all. They seem somewhat distant for a newly married couple, don't you think?"

"Maybe it's because they're around the parents—or maybe it's because of this business trouble. Never mind Kendra's looks, nothing's tougher on a marriage than money problems."

"Spoken from experience."

"Very much from experience, yes."

She moved closer. "Money certainly doesn't interfere with us."

"You're right. You've got it. I don't. It's very simple."

She was in his arms. "There are other attractions."

"Which is why I might demonstrate one of those attractions right now."

"You think that's an attraction?"

"Why don't we find out?"

"With the kids in the other room?"

"They're not kids, they're adults," Tree said. "We'll be quiet. I'll grit my teeth."

He kissed her.

7

The next morning Tree parked the Beetle on the ocean side of Captiva Drive, choosing a spot that provided a good view of the front gates at the Traven mansion.

The last time he had been to the house, he had driven straight through those gates and walked up the steep staircase to the front entrance. Jorge, the Travens' majordomo, had poured him coffee. Now here he was huddled incongruously on a roadside, trying not to be noticed.

And waiting.

In the days after Brand Traven's surprise release from prison, reporters and cameramen had camped outside, creating worse traffic jams than usual along Captiva. But the former media mogul had known exactly how to thwart the press dogs who once served him: he simply refused to show his face, starving the gluttony of the twenty-four hour news machine. The machine could not function without movement. The reporters soon departed in search of easier prey. This morning, no cameramen lingered out front. No TV trucks were parked along the beach side of the road. There were no gawking tourists with digital cameras, no police grimly rerouting traffic.

Only private detective Tree Callister on the job, sitting behind the wheel of the Beetle sipping a lukewarm café latte, listening to old rock and roll on the radio—something he swore he was going to stop doing any day now.

The gates at the Traven house began to swing open. A Cadillac Escalade came out onto the roadway, headed south toward Sanibel Island. Tree caught a glimpse of Brand Traven behind the wheel.

Tree swung the Beetle onto the road and sped after him. He kept Traven in sight as he turned onto Tarpon Bay Road and then onto Periwinkle Way. He drove as far as the Tahitian Mall.

Tree watched Traven park his vehicle in the mall, get out, lock it, and then lumber up a flight of stairs to the walkway that ringed the building. He moved slowly, bent forward as though against a strong wind. He wore a short-sleeved shirt and rumpled linen slacks. He looked more like a retiree on a pension than an international media mogul who once hobnobbed with the world's most powerful men and women.

Traven entered a store at the end of the walkway, Adventures in Paradise. Tree parked and waited.

The Beetle's passenger door flew open, and a figure squeezed into the car's interior. The Beetle could barely contain the hulking form of Ferne Clowers.

She said, "You've got the wrong idea about me."

"What are you doing here?" Tree replied, sounding a lot calmer than he was.

"I just wanted you to know—" her voice choked, as if overwhelmed by her emotions. "That thing up at Matlacha? That was a mistake, and I'm sorry. It won't happen again."

"Does that mean you're not going to shoot me?"

"No, I'm not," she said definitively.

"I can't tell you how relieved I am to hear that," Tree said.

"I'm not a bad person, Tree," she continued. "People have misconceptions about me."

"What misconceptions do they have, Ferne?"

"That I am a really bad person."

"Maybe it has something to do with the way you act."

"I am trying to change my behavior, Tree, I truly am. More than anyone else, you helped me understand how important it is to make real changes in my life."

"But why did you want to shoot me in the first place?"

"It was a mistake," she repeated.

"A mistake? Ferne, you lured me over to Matlacha. You had Slippery waiting on that shrimp boat with a gun. If it had gone off the way it was supposed to, I'd be dead."

"I can't tell you how bad I feel about that."

Before he could do anything, she leaned over and kissed him hard on the mouth. He was so surprised he just sat there as she worked her lips against his. Then she tore herself away, tears rolling down her cheeks. She fumbled for the door handle.

"Goodbye, Tree."

She was gone out the door, a big slump-shouldered thing showing more grace than he might have expected, hurrying across the parking lot.

He sat still, not moving, his mouth tingling. He looked around the Tahitian Mall. Sometime during his encounter with Ferne, Brand Traven had left.

He took out his cell phone. It seemed to take Cee Jay Boone forever to come on the line.

"I'm not supposed to be talking to you," she said.

"I'm at the Tahitian Mall on Periwinkle Way," Tree said. "Ferne Clowers was just here."

"There is no Ferne Clowers," Cee Jay said. "No such name shows up on any police data base."

"Whoever she is, she got in my car just now."

"And she didn't shoot you?" Cee Jay sounded disappointed.

"Not this time, no. Look, the point is, she just left. If you get over here, maybe you can catch her."

For a couple of long beats, Cee Jay didn't say anything. "Are you there?" Tree said.

"Yes, I'm here. Did she say anything to you?"

"She said it was a mistake, trying to kill me. She said she was sorry. Then she—" Tree's voice trailed off.

"Then she what?"

"She kissed me."

"Okay, Tree, what are you doing here?" Cee Jay, exasperated.

"Maybe the next time she shows up, she doesn't feel like kissing me. Maybe the next time she's inclined to shoot me again. This woman is crazy, and she's got a gun, and for whatever reason, she's stalking me."

"All right. Stay where you are. I'll get a squad car over there."

8

An hour after two uniformed Sanibel officers finally arrived to take his statement, Tree, still rattled by his encounter with Ferne Clowers, decided that was enough private detecting for one day, and drove home.

Chris's Dodge was not in the drive when Tree arrived at the house, but Kendra's was. He went inside and got a Diet Coke out of the fridge. He stood in the kitchen taking a long, reviving swig, hearing a voice from the terrace. He crossed the kitchen and slid the glass door open.

"I don't give a damn what she says." Kendra was saying. "Sasha, listen to me. This is bullshit. Okay? I'm still dealing with this. That's part of the reason I'm here. All right, but let me talk to her."

Tree went out onto the terrace. Kendra, wearing a wisp of black thong, was stretched out on a chaise lounge, her iPhone pressed to her ear.

"I'll have to call you back." She dropped the iPhone onto the chaise lounge and lifted herself up on one elbow, removing her sunglasses. She gave one of the lazy smiles that must have inspired *Playboy* readers all over the world. Or maybe it wasn't the smile.

"Hey," Tree said.

"I hope you don't mind," she said.

"Mind what?"

"Me being topless. Doesn't bother you, Papa Tree?"

"No, of course not." Then he added dumbly: "It's Florida."

She lay back on the lounge, replacing the sunglasses, her body glistening.

"Are you through private detecting for the day, Papa Tree?" The way she said "Papa Tree" made him sound like the title character in a children's book: *The Adventures of Papa Tree.*

"Do you want anything?"

"I'm fine, thanks. Are you going to sit out here?"

"I'm just having a Diet Coke." He held up the Coke can as if it was evidence he was telling the truth.

"Doesn't that stuff rot your teeth or kill brain cells or something?"

"Don't tell me that. It's the only vice I have left."

She laughed, and he sat in an adjacent chair. "Where's Chris?"

"Out. Somewhere. I don't know."

Tree sipped at his Coke, and made a point of studying the robot Pool Rover chugging around the edge of the swimming pool.

"Are the two of you okay?"

The question caused her to sit up and once again remove the sunglasses. "What would make you say that, Papa Tree?"

"So the two of you are okay?"

"Depends on your definition of 'okay,' I suppose. You know, we're a married couple. We have our ups and downs."

"Chris seems to be drinking a lot," Tree said.

She sat back on the lounge, using a hand to fan herself. "Chris needs to get a grip. Everything's going to be fine. We just have to get through this, that's all."

"So something is wrong."

She turned her gaze toward him, blue eyes shining, delivering another of her killer smiles. "I can't thank you enough for letting us stay with you and Freddie, Papa Tree. It's good to get out of Chicago for a while, sit in the sun. Relax."

"Tell me something, Kendra," Tree said. "Why do you call me Papa Tree?"

"You don't like it when I call you that?"

"I didn't say that."

"Makes you feel old, huh?"

"Yeah, I guess it does."

"You being a private detective and everything."

"It has nothing to do with that."

"Doesn't it?" She swung her legs off the chaise lounge. He tried to keep his eyes averted. "I mean, isn't that what the detective thing is about? Trying to beat age, stay young?"

Tree said defensively, "I hadn't thought of it that way."

"But isn't it?"

"Kendra, you have a marvelous way of deflecting questions," he said.

"Do I? Or maybe it's just that you're not hearing what you want to hear."

"What do you think I want to hear?"

"You don't want to hear me calling you Papa Tree, that's for sure." She trained those blue eyes on him. "I see you looking at me. I know what you're thinking."

"No Kendra," he said firmly. "You don't know what I'm thinking."

She grinned and then got up from the lounge, the Chicago goddess blazing in the sun. "Tree, I'm going inside for a shower. Great talking to you."

He watched her saunter off across the pool deck. Freddie was right. She did have a tramp stamp.

A red, red rose.

My love is like a red, red rose, Tree thought. Robbie Burns, wasn't it?

Chris didn't come home for dinner. Kendra appeared unconcerned as they sat at the glass-topped table on the terrace and ate the orange roughy and asparagus Freddie had prepared. Kendra smiled at Freddie and said how good the fish was. She usually wasn't that crazy about fish. But this was fantastic.

Chris still had not appeared by the time Freddie and Tree went into their bedroom leaving Kendra watching David Letterman. "Are you worried?" Freddie asked once they were settled in bed.

"I wish I knew what was wrong," Tree said.

"Maybe nothing is wrong. Other than a little old-fashioned marital stress."

"You think that's what it is?"

"Don't you?"

"Does Kendra say anything to you?"

"Kendra thinks she makes you nervous."

He thought about their unsettling afternoon encounter. She claimed to know what he was thinking, and she might be right—*that* made him nervous.

Aloud, he said, "It is hard to know how to behave when you come home and find your daughter-in-law sunbathing topless, but that's not the real problem."

"What's the real problem?"

"I wish I knew. Chris won't talk about it and neither will she. She thinks they'll get through all right; Chris isn't so certain, I don't think."

"Well, I'm going to sleep," Freddie said. "I've got an early morning meeting. Incidentally, how did you do with Brand Traven today?"

He thought of telling her about Ferne Clowers and then decided against it. "He went shopping."

"No mistress?"

"Not so far."

She kissed him. "And quit worrying. Chris and Kendra will get it figured out."

He worried only until the moment he fell asleep.

The next morning when he got up with Freddie, he padded into the kitchen and made her coffee. He looked out the kitchen window and saw Chris's SUV in the drive. He had arrived home sometime during the night. Tree felt relieved—the father concerned about the late-arriving son, just like it was when Chris was a teenager.

How little it changes, Tree thought. Chris was home and safe. Everything was all right. Chris and his wife were here for a visit. No more than that.

9

On Monday, Brand Traven drove to the Sanibel Island Bookshop. The owner, Hollie Schmid, later told Tree that Traven had purchased a copy of *A Tale of Two Cities*. Traven then drove to Jerry's Foods Center where he bought ice cream at PocoLoco. Then he went home.

Tuesday, Tree followed him off island to the Tanger Mall. He visited the Ralph Lauren store and emerged with two shopping bags. He then went into the Nike store, followed by a visit to the Famous Footwear Outlet.

Wednesday, he spent an hour browsing at MacIntosh Books and Paper. The owner, Susie Holly, refused to tell Tree what the media mogul purchased. At the Lazy Flamingo around one o'clock, Traven sat at the bar eating a grouper sandwich and drinking a Diet Coke. He spoke to the bartender, but otherwise kept to himself. None of the customers appeared to recognize their infamous luncheon companion. Traven drove home at three o'clock.

Thursday, he never left the house. Friday, Elizabeth Traven called Tree and said she wanted to see him. They agreed to meet at one o'clock, at the Edison Restaurant on McGregor Boulevard.

Tree waited in the dark-bricked lobby beneath a formal black and white portrait of Thomas Edison. He decided the old man looked uncomfortable in his formal getup, presiding over herds of smartly dressed young women who drank free vodka at the Edison every Wednesday night, and who doubtless challenged the old man's conservative view of things.

Elizabeth Traven made her entrance a few minutes later, looking unusually pale. There were dark circles beneath her eyes. Tree wondered if she was getting enough sleep. "I've been away," she said curtly as if that explained her exhausted appearance. She did not choose to tell him where.

They sat on the porch overlooking the Fort Myers Country Club. Elizabeth wore a linen jacket over a white blouse tucked into carefully faded jeans. She ordered a gin and tonic from the waiter. Tree said, "You're in your Thomas Edison phase."

She looked at him with tired eyes.

"The Ford and Edison Winter Estates. Now the Edison restaurant."

"I told you. I was going to write a book about Edison."

"I thought it was Ford."

She waved a dismissive hand. "Whatever." The waiter arrived with her gin.

She took a long sip that had the effect of putting a little more color in her cheeks. "So what have you got for me, Mr. Callister?"

"Not much."

She frowned. "Not much?"

"You're in the house with him, you must know."

"I told you, I've been away," she said. "That's why I don't know what my husband's been up to. That's why I hired you."

"He went shopping, that's as interesting as it's gotten."

She gave him a sharp look. "Shopping? Where did he go shopping?"

"A number of places around the island."

"Name one."

"Okay. The first day he drove to the Tahitian Gardens mall. A place called Adventures in Paradise."

"What did he buy?"

"I don't know."

"That's not much help."

"What do you expect me to do? Stop him and demand to see what he's carrying?"

"I expect results," she snapped.

When he didn't respond, she sighed and pursed her mouth.

"Understand this about Brand," Elizabeth said. "Brand does not shop. He never shops."

"Well, he was shopping the other day. Maybe he needed a pair of socks. They've got nice socks at Adventures in Paradise. I don't know."

"He doesn't need socks. He doesn't need anything. At least nothing you buy in a store."

Tree looked at her more closely. "You don't really think he's having an affair, do you?"

She said, "I think he's trying to kill me."

Tree gave her a long look before he said, "Are you serious?"

"Of course I'm serious. Why would I say something like that if I wasn't serious?"

Tree lowered his voice to ensure no one at the nearby tables overheard him. "You really think your husband is trying to kill you."

"No, Mr. Callister. I'm just making it up because I want to have lunch with you."

"Why? Why would he want you dead?"

"Presumably he doesn't like me anymore," she said with a shrug, as if all disliked wives were subject to murder plots.

"Come on, Mrs. Traven."

"Why does anyone kill anyone? I haven't a clue. The fact is my husband wants to kill me."

"Then you should go to the police."

She rolled her eyes. "No police. Not for the moment. I prefer to do it this way. You keep an eye on him until we know what he's up to. If it turns out I'm right, then we go to the police."

"If you really think he's going to hurt you, Mrs. Traven, you shouldn't take any chances."

She gave him a sweet smile. "I've got you to protect me, Mr. Callister."

"If you're messing with me, Mrs. Traven, I will walk away from this," Tree said.

She reacted with a dismissive snort. "Don't be ridiculous. You won't do anything of the sort. Why should you? You're being well paid. You don't have any other clients. What's more, if you did walk away and something happened to me, how would you feel?"

"Guilt-stricken for the rest of my life, I'm sure," Tree said.

"There you go. I'll phone you in a couple of days for an update."

She started up. "You haven't finished your drink," he said.

Elizabeth gave him a dark look before she marched away.

10

"That was the same year I dated Joan Crawford." Rex Baxter was holding court at the end of the bar at the Lighthouse Restaurant.

One of his young listeners said, "Who's Joan Crawford?"

"Big Hollywood movie star in the thirties and forties," Todd Jackson said.

The young listener looked at him blankly.

"Of course, she wasn't so big when I met her," Rex said. "She was older then, but she still looked great. I was a kid, just arrived in Hollywood. It was the last gasp of the studio system. Universal Studios had hired a bunch of us youngsters to be part of a talent program, hoping to turn us into movie stars. Clint Eastwood was in it, but they threw him out. Go figure.

"I met Joan one night at Chasen's. She saw me at the bar and came over. We got to talking. A little older, a few wrinkles, but she had great skin. I remember that about her. Soft, white skin. Hell, she was Joan Crawford. I was dazzled."

"Joan Crawford," said the young listener, as though attempting to twist his tongue around a foreign name.

"Anyway, Chasen's is closing for the night—back then they rolled up the streets in Beverly Hills at eleven o'clock. Maybe they still do. So Joan suggests I come back to her place for a nightcap. That's what you had in those days. Not a drink. A nightcap.

"We drive into the Hills to Joan's place. It's dark and we go inside, and she doesn't turn on any lights. She excuses herself, and I'm left alone, kind of stumbling around in the dark, wondering what's going to happen. Time goes by, and there's no sign of Joan, and I'm starting to get a little worried. Eventually, I open the door I had seen her disappear through, and I find myself in a sitting room. There's a fire burning in this huge fireplace even though it's summer. Lying in front of the fireplace on a fur rug is Joan Crawford—naked. She looks at me, smiles, and says, 'What took you so long?'"

The small circle surrounding Rex chuckled and applauded. Rex beamed. Rex in his element, Tree reflected, lost in the vast palace of his past, rediscovering its nooks and crannies, luxuriating in its warm afterglow. Who could blame him? In the past, you were always the star; you always made the right move, ended up on the fur rug in front of the fireplace with the famous woman.

Only the present let you down. No wonder the older you got, the more you tended to retreat into your past, arranging it into wonderfully recalled anecdotes. He did the same thing, just not tonight. Tonight he had characters named Slippery on his trail and beautiful women with opaque eyes and steely determination handing him envelopes stuffed with cash. No time for the past with a present like this.

Not far away, Ray Dayton leaned next to Freddie. He'd had what the Ray Man liked to call "a couple of drinks." That was not a good thing, particularly when Mrs. Ray wasn't present, as she wasn't this evening. Ray had his eyes on Kendra who had just entered on Chris's arm. She wore a plain white blouse strategically unbuttoned to remind interested parties of the two reasons she had been chosen as a *Playboy* magazine Playmate. It wasn't just the Ray Man's eyes, either. Everyone in the bar watched her hungrily.

"I can think a lot more about process and planning as soon as I get rid of the house," Ray said to Freddie.

"The place on Woodring Road," Freddie said.

"I never should have bought it," Ray said.

"I told you not to."

"Now if I sell the damned thing, I take a loss. I hate that. I hate losing at anything."

Kendra came over and pecked Tree on the cheek and said, "Papa Tree." She glanced at the Ray Man who immediately looked nervous.

She grinned at him until Freddie made introductions. "So you're Freddie's boss," Kendra said. She did not take her eyes off him.

"I'm not sure," Ray said. "Someone once said power is something you have until you try to use it. With Freddie, I'm discovering how true that is."

Everyone laughed,

"I'm going to the little girls' room," Kendra said.

Freddie came and stood beside Tree. "What was that all about?"

"What?"

"Kendra and Ray."

"It's Friday night. The Ray Man is being the Ray Man."

"It felt as though they knew one another."

"How could they?" Tree said. "She's never been down here before."

"Funny, that's all," Freddie said.

He watched Rex in action and smiled fondly.

"What are you thinking?" Freddie asked.

"I was thinking about how many times I've heard Rex tell the Joan Crawford story."

"Is it true?"

"As true as the Rita Hayworth story."

"There's a Rita Hayworth story?"

"He had an affair with her in Rome. The older Rita, mind you. The Rita suffering early signs of dementia."

"Quite the stud for the older broads in his day, our Rex," Freddie said.

Tree followed her gaze to where Kendra had begun to dance with Ray Dayton.

"That was fast," Tree said.

"You see? They do know one another."

"That's impossible," Tree said.

The song ended. Freddie looked relieved, and then tensed again as Ray and Kendra remained in place. The keyboard player started on "The Wind Beneath My Wings." Kendra drifted into Ray Dayton's arms. Tree looked around for Chris, but couldn't see him.

"Let's dance," Freddie said. It came out like a marching order.

"Because I am the wind beneath your wings?"

"I want to keep an eye on Ray."

"In case he starts to tear Kendra's clothes off?"

"He's like all men," Freddie said.

"Weak?"

"And stupid where women are concerned. Speaking of which, how are you doing with Brand Traven?"

"It's his wife I'm concerned about."

Freddie raised her eyebrows. "Oh?"

"Now she thinks her husband is trying to kill her."

"She told you this?"

"At lunch."

"I thought she suspected he was having an affair."

"That was yesterday. Today, he's going to kill her."

"What do you think?"

"Well, there is not a whole lot of evidence he is having an affair."

"What makes Elizabeth so sure he's trying to kill her?"

"She doesn't say, but she wants me out there watching him."

"I don't trust her," Freddie said. "And you are far too enamored of her."

"Enamored? There's a word I haven't heard for a while."

"I'm an old-fashioned girl," Freddie said.

"And I am not, as you say, enamored of her."

Freddie gave him a look before becoming distracted by the sight of Ray moving Kendra awkwardly around. They looked like they were at a country dance in a John Ford western. Kendra giggled at something Ray said. His face reddened.

"Good grief," Freddie said. "He's blushing."

"The power of Kendra," Tree said.

"The Wind Beneath My Wings" ended. Kendra gave the Ray Man one of her two hundred thousand watt smiles and planted a sisterly kiss on his cheek. Except Tree doubted many men would consider a kiss from Kendra "sisterly."

He led Freddie back toward the bar. Chris, glass in hand, threw his free arm around his father. "Dad," he said with a crooked grin.

In the background, Tree heard Rex Baxter say, "Did you see *To Hell And Back*? The Audie Murphy story? I was in that with Audie."

Another voice said, "Who's Audie Murphy?"

Exactly, thought Tree. That was the problem with old stories in this new world. No one knew who you were talking about.

"Dad, I think I really screwed up." Chris stood in front of him, his face flushed and anxious.

"What do you mean? What did you screw up, Chris?"

"Everything," Chris said. "Every damned thing imaginable."

Kendra materialized beside her husband, wrapping a possessive arm around his waist. "Time to go home, baby boy."

Chris managed another lopsided grin. "I think my beautiful wife wants me to keep my big mouth shut. Isn't that right, honey? Isn't that what you'd like me to do?"

"What I'd like you to do is to stop drinking and get a good night's sleep." Kendra spoke in a reasonable voice, but it contained a warning edge.

"If I keep talking I'm just going to get us in trouble, aren't I?"

Kendra gave Tree an exasperated look. "Maybe you can do something with him, Papa Tree. I certainly can't."

"We're all tired, Chris," Tree said to his son. "It's time to go home."

"Sure, sure," Chris said. "Let's go home. Let's be a big happy family together. Happy, happy family."

Yes, they could be that, all right, Tree thought.

Except they weren't.

11

Monday, Tree spent much of the morning outside the Traven mansion wondering if Brand was home.

Then about eleven o'clock his Escalade shot onto Captiva Drive, moving so fast it startled Tree. Tree got the Beetle started and went after him.

Traven slowed coming off Sanibel Island and then picked up speed once he was on the causeway. Off the causeway, he turned left onto McGregor Boulevard and followed it until it became Tamiami Trail.

Then Traven really put the pedal to the metal as he headed north. Tree pressed the Beetle forward, but the little car didn't respond well. Tree could hardly blame the Beetle. It was used to puttering around Sanibel and Captiva, not being forced to race along a freeway at top speed.

Traven swept ahead exhibiting the same aggressive tendencies he must have brought to the operation of his media empire. Tree had not seen that exuberance until now; life as just another convict at Coleman prison had made him seem somehow diminished.

Here was the real Brand, working at full speed, sweeping over the wide Caloosahatchee and Peace rivers, past Punta Gorda, not pausing at Port Charlotte to gaze at the gulf islands but turning north on I-75, hardly ever leaving the passing lane or taking his foot off the gas pedal, impatient, a force of nature on the move.

Tree thought he might stop at Sarasota, but he didn't even slow down. Perhaps Tampa, "a great city for twenty-somethings." Where had he read that? Travern didn't fit the description, however, and so on he went, continuing his flight north, turning inland, passing Wesley Chapel, and then crossing the causeways at Moody Lake and McClendon Lake.

The initial adrenalin-producing high induced by Traven's first real movement began to wear off and Tree found the beating sun and the flat, unchanging landscape were making him drowsy. He bounced up and down on the seat, snapped his fingers, and turned up the volume of the radio so that Roy Orbison filled the car with "Pretty Woman."

Suddenly, it struck him where Traven was headed. That woke him up. It couldn't be. Why would he be driving to Coleman Correctional, the place from which he so recently had been released? It didn't make sense.

But as Traven swung off the turnpike onto Country Road 470 and then accelerated onto Highway 310, it became apparent that's exactly where he was headed.

He whipped past the Sumterville Cemetery, making a hard right in a cloud of dust and gravel onto County Road 470. The sprawling white smudge of Coleman Correctional popped into view.

Tree watched Traven turn onto NE Terrace, the road leading to the complex, and decided he would almost certainly be noticed if he followed him.

He pulled off beneath a grove of trees not far from a sign warning that there was no trespassing on prison property.

The trees provided little protection from the heat. Tree feared the Beetle's engine would overheat, and so he shut it off. Even with the windows down, he could hardly breathe. He got out and went over and slumped under a tree. He caught the merciful whisper of a breeze. That was better. He stretched out, his back braced against the trunk. Just for a moment, he thought. Just for a moment, I'll close my eyes.

———————

He jerked awake, smacking his lips, sitting up. How long had he been out?

He looked at his watch. It was past two. He had been asleep for at least fifteen minutes, time enough for Traven to have driven away.

Damn! What kind of detective was he, anyway? The stupid, sleepy kind, apparently.

Tree jumped to his feet just as Traven's Escalade arrived at the intersection. He barely paused before veering onto 470, headed back the way he had come.

Someone was beside him. Brand Traven had picked up a passenger at Coleman Correctional.

12

Traven arrived back in Fort Myers at five o'clock. Instead of going straight to Sanibel Island, however, he took San Carlos Boulevard and crossed the bridge to Fort Myers Beach.

He came along Estero as far as the Lani Kai Resort, a massive aqua green edifice with a fading American flag painted above a mural of a waterfall and tropical palms.

Traven maneuvered the Escalade up a ramp beneath a portico. Tree saw the passenger get out carrying a black suitcase. He walked toward a covered walkway.

Tree drove across the street and found a parking spot. By the time he ran back to the hotel, the Escalade was gone.

Native girls in grass skirts swayed across a mural on either side of the walkway. Halfway along, a staircase led up to the lobby.

Traven's passenger was at the reception desk with his back to Tree talking to the female receptionist. The suitcase was at his feet. The passenger was African American, large and well-muscled in a rumpled dark suit that looked out of place at the Lani Kai.

Not wanting to hang around and attract attention, Tree went back down to the walkway. A red-shirted security guard eyed him suspiciously: old guy in this hotel? What was *that* all about?

Tree was debating what to do when Traven's passenger abruptly appeared in the walkway and headed toward the beach. An outside bar area was jammed with muscular young guys, bare-chested, drinking beer as they cheered a quartet of young women in string bikinis, dancing on pushed-together picnic tables.

The amplified voice of a master of ceremonies announced that voting was about to commence for finalists in the booty shaking contest. Tree kept his eye on the passenger as he leaned an elbow against the bar. He seemed as out of place here as, well, as Tree.

Traven's passenger ordered a beer. When the bartender brought it, the passenger threw dollar bills on the bar and then tilted his head back and took a long swallow, drinking straight from the can. It looked as though it had been a long time since he'd had a beer.

Tree turned to face the broad back of a teenager with a shaved head and a mass of tattooed snakes weaving around a large skull emblazoned with "Survival of the Sickest." Wait till you turn sixty, Tree thought. You may regret the day you had that done.

The crowd hollered its approval as one of the young women on the picnic tables worked herself into an impressive frenzy as she demonstrated why they called it booty shaking.

When Tree pulled his eyes away to search for Traven's passenger, he had disappeared. Tree edged around the crowd and then turned to scan the beach just as a couple walked hand in hand around a golf cart advertising dolphin tours and wave runner rentals.

Tree recognized Ray Dayton first, his white linen shirt open to the waist to show off a sunburned chest.

Kendra Callister, the woman whose hand he held, wore sunglasses and a tank top. The sunglasses were her attempt at disguise. The tank top was the evidence of the disguise's failure.

13

Tree instinctively stepped back, right into the teenager with the snakes and skull tattoos. The kid gave him a dirty look. Ray and Kendra, still holding hands, moved briskly into the walkway.

The announcer informed the cheering crowd that three booty shaking finalists had been chosen. Ray never glanced back. Tree guessed that when you were with Kendra Callister, you weren't much concerned with who won a booty shaking contest.

Still holding hands, the couple continued through the walkway, up some steps and then down into the courtyard where Ray had parked his Lexus. He held the door open so Kendra could slip inside. Tree watched the Lexus pull onto Estero Boulevard. He ran across the street to his car.

The late afternoon traffic streamed off the island and snaked onto the bridge. For a time Tree couldn't see the Ray Man's car. But then he came over the bridge's crest and spotted it on San Carlos Boulevard.

The previous evening he had argued that Kendra and Ray could not possibly know each other. More evidence he should always listen to Freddie. Of course, there could be any number of reasonable explanations for Freddie's boss and his daughter-in-law leaving the Lani Kai Island Resort together. He just could not think of what those reasonable explanations might be.

He caught up to the Lexus as it swung onto Summerlin. The Ray Man drove leisurely, in no rush to get anywhere, happy, apparently, to be in the company of the wondrous Kendra.

To Tree's surprise, they drove to Dayton's Supermarket. The Ray Man parked, and they got out together. He walked Kendra to where she had left her Dodge Durango. She leaned against the hood, so that Ray could avidly kiss her mouth. She returned the kiss. As avidly? Tree thought not, although at this distance, it was hard to tell.

Ray opened the door for her. Kendra blessed him with one of her most impressive smiles and then climbed inside. He watched as she drove out of the parking lot. When she was on Periwinkle Way, the Ray Man performed a curious little march into the store.

From his vantage point on the shoulder of Periwinkle Way where he had stopped the Beetle, Tree wondered if Freddie might have seen this little drama unfolding from inside the store. He looked at his watch. It was getting close to seven. She was home by now and wondering where he was. He debated what to do next. It didn't take much investigative prowess to imagine Kendra driving to Andy Rosse Lane and a quiet evening with her husband and in-laws. He could go back to the Lani Kai and Brand Traven's mysterious passenger, but he had no heart for it.

Home, then.

Kendra was just getting out of her Dodge when he pulled into the drive.

She gave him the same dazzling smile she had provided Ray. "Hey, Papa Tree. What are you doing? Following me?"

"It's a possibility," Tree said with more seriousness than he intended.

"I'm a pretty boring person to be following around," she said breezily.

"I didn't think you knew Ray Dayton," Tree said.

She did not blink before she said, "I don't."

"Funny, at the Lighthouse I got the impression the two of you had met before."

Kendra smiled and said, "I'm going to jump into the shower."

To wash off the Ray Man? Tree wondered.

They went inside together and found Freddie in the kitchen tossing a salad. She had changed from her work clothes into shorts and a T-shirt. He kissed her on the mouth and held her tight. Kendra disappeared into the guest bedroom.

"Are you all right?" she said.

"I'm not all right because I hug you?"

"Because I've been married to you a long time and can sense certain things."

"Such as?"

"Such as when you are not all right."

"I'm fine."

She gave him a look and then went back to tossing the salad. He had debated on the way home about what to tell Freddie and decided, for the moment, to say nothing. Despite what he had seen, he could be getting it wrong.

He tried to imagine that kiss in the parking lot as an act of friendship. He doubted friendship had much to do with it.

"You haven't heard from Chris, have you?" he said to Freddie.

"Nothing. Where do they both disappear to?"

Kendra could be found afternoons at the Lani Kai Hotel, Tree thought.

He heard Kendra finish her shower and then return to the guest bedroom. Twenty minutes later, there was the sound of the back door closing. Tree glanced out the kitchen window in time to see Kendra pulling out of the drive. Freddie stood beside him.

"I say again: where do they go?"

"Beats me," Tree said.

Thirty minutes later, Chris arrived home. He'd been drinking again, a little uncertain on his feet, trying to pretend he was okay. He did not ask about Kendra.

They ate a tense dinner on the terrace, the salad accompanied by Freddie's turkey burgers with fresh basil, sun-dried tomatoes and crumbled goat cheese. Or Tree and Freddie ate. Chris pushed his food around.

Tree strained to make conversation. Freddie strained right back. Chris didn't even make the attempt. After dinner, he retreated to the guest room. Freddie looked at Tree but said nothing. Tree cleaned up the dishes and then joined Freddie in the TV room.

Tree and Freddie watched CNN. Tree said he couldn't decide whether he liked Piers Morgan. They watched *The Good Wife*. Tree had no trouble deciding he liked the lawyer drama starring Julianna Margulies. Freddie liked it, too, but not enough to stop her dozing on the sofa.

At eleven, just as he was about to awaken Freddie so they could go to bed, the telephone rang. Freddie stirred. Tree went into the kitchen and picked up the phone.

When he said, "hello" there was nothing but the sound of someone breathing. He almost hung up before a voice said, "I don't think I'm all right."

"What?" Tree said. "Who is this?"

"Tree," Elizabeth Traven said. "Tree, are you there?"

"Mrs. Traven?"

Silence on the line.

"Mrs. Traven?"

"I—"

The line went dead.

14

He replaced the receiver. Freddie sat up, yawning. "What's wrong?"

"I just got a weird call from Elizabeth Traven," Tree said. "I'm wondering whether to go over there."

Freddie got to her feet, stretching. "Why don't you call her back first?"

He dialed her number. The phone rang four times before the voice mail clicked on. Tree hung up. "No answer," he said. "I'm going over."

"Do you want me to come with you?"

"No, I'm sure it's all right. I just want to make sure."

"Be careful," Freddie said.

He was turning onto Captiva Drive before he realized he had forgotten his cell phone. Never mind. He could phone Freddie from the Traven house. When he got there, he found the front gates wide open. He drove through and parked below the main staircase. He took the steps two at a time. At the top of the stairs, the muscles in his stomach began to tighten—the front door was ajar.

He pushed the door further open and stepped into the interior. The foyer was cast in shadow. He crossed, expecting to be accosted by Jorge, the house majordomo. But then he remembered Jorge had left. When you were no longer rich, the help was the first to go. He came down into the vast dimness of the living room.

"Mrs. Traven?" he called. "Mrs. Traven? Are you here?"

Through the floor-to-ceiling windows Tree could see moonlight reflected off the waves on San Carlos Bay. The moonlight captured the lump of a body sprawled across the white sofa. Except the sofa was no longer white but stained black. The black flowed out of the gashes in Brand Traven's chest; it flowed away from the silver scissors protruding from the base of his throat.

Tree stood there in shock, staring at the black horror on the sofa. He took a step. "Mr. Traven," he said.

Traven's eyes were open, but there was no life in them. Lying there in a sea of black, Traven seemed a hollow husk of himself, his mouth yawning open, as though something had escaped—his soul perhaps?

Tree looked around. On the floor beside the sofa lay a scrunched-up ball of cardboard. Had Traven dropped it when he was attacked? Tree picked the ball off the floor and opened it. It was a business card.

There was nothing on it but a single red rose.

He heard movement coming from the back of the house.

Still holding the card, he got to his feet, head cocked at an angle.

Listening.

The sound of a door closing.

He went over to the window. Below, outlined in moonlight, a figure crossed the lawn, headed toward the ocean. Man or woman? He couldn't tell.

Then, as abruptly it appeared in the moonlight, the figure evaporated into the darkness.

15

"According to my partner, you do this a lot," Detective Own Markfield said.

"Do what?" Tree was sitting with Markfield at a dainty white table on the lawn at the rear of the Traven mansion. This was where not so long ago he had shared coffee with Elizabeth Traven. Where was she tonight? he wondered. The grieving wife should be here, weeping over the body of her fallen husband.

"You turn up at murder scenes," Markfield said. "We keep finding you in the vicinity of dead bodies."

Markfield did not sound happy about it. Tree could not blame him.

He glanced around, marveling once again at the sheer numbers of official-looking people who showed up at a crime scene: local uniformed police; members of the Crime Scene Investigation Unit of the Lee County Sheriff's Department; a couple of assistant district attorneys sent over by the Lee County district attorney; a forensics team from Fort Myers, as well as half a dozen detectives from that department. A small army dedicated to discovering Brand Traven's killer, and Tree Callister was momentarily at its epicenter.

"Where is Cee Jay, incidentally?" Tree asked.

"The department has decided that it's better if Detective Boone concentrate on other cases," Markfield said in a formal voice.

"Tell Cee Jay I miss her," Tree said.

"Let's just go over a few things." Markfield brushed a hand over his gold-highlighted hair. Somehow it retained its perfection at one o'clock in the morning. "Mrs. Traven is a client. Is that correct?"

"Yes," Tree said.

"You mean to tell me Elizabeth Traven engaged *you*?" Markfield sounded incredulous.

"Why is that so surprising?" Tree said.

Instead of answering, Markfield said, "Was there something going on between the two of you?"

"Between Mrs. Traven and myself? You've got to be kidding."

"All right, Mrs. Traven hired you," Markfield went on. "To do what, exactly?"

"She wanted me to follow her husband."

"He was just out of prison," Markfield said. "Why would she want him followed?"

"Why do most women want their husbands followed?" Tree sounding like the world-weary gumshoe who had seen it all.

"Fill me in, Tree," Markfield said. "Why do women have their husbands followed?"

"Initially, she thought he was having an affair."

"Did she say with whom?"

"That's what she wanted me to find out."

Markfield looked at him hard. "Initially?"

"Then it was because she thought he was going to kill her."

There was a long pause before Markfield said, "And was he?"

"Was he trying to kill her?"

"Was he having an affair?"

"Not as far as I could see."

"How about murder? Any evidence he was trying to kill her?"

"No," Tree said.

"So when she called you tonight—"

"It sounded as though she was in trouble," Tree said.

"Because of what she previously had told you."

"That's right."

"Except that when you got here, it was Brand Traven who was dead, not his wife," Markfield said.

"As it turned out."

"Any idea where Mrs. Traven is at this moment?"

"No," Tree said.

Markfield gave him a skeptical look. "You're sure about that?"

"I don't know where she is."

"And you haven't tried to get in touch with her?"

Funny, it had not even crossed his mind. He shook his head.

"Okay, you came in the house and found the body. What happened after that?"

"Like I told the other officers: I heard something. A door closing. Something, I'm not sure. I went to the window and saw a person running across the lawn. Toward the water."

"But you couldn't see who it was?"

"No."

"Man or woman?"

"I couldn't tell."

"But it could have been a woman?"

"It could have been a man," Tree answered.

Markfield said something about lots of press waiting outside. He said he didn't want Tree speaking to anyone. Officers would drive him home. They would drop off his car later. He went along without complaint. He felt numb, without emotion.

A few minutes later he was in the back of a police cruiser making its way through the crush of reporters and cameramen outside the Traven house.

Faces flashed against the windows, mouths opening and closing, expelling words he could not make out. Lights exploded. Then the crowds and the lights were gone, and there was the sound of rushing air and an occasional blast of static from the police radio. The two officers in front said nothing. He stared at the backs of their heads. Then he fished the wrinkled business card out of his pocket—the card he should have shown Detective Owen Markfield but didn't. Light shadows flicked across the red rose.

Where had he seen that before?

Kendra.

Her tramp stamp. Trying to keep his eyes off that tramp stamp. Was it the same? It certainly looked similar. Or did thousands of young women wear similar tattoos on their lower backs?

He put the card back in his pocket as the police cruiser pulled into the drive at Andy Rosse Lane. Freddie met him on the walkway. She embraced him, holding him tight. Dimly he was aware of the police car pulling out of the drive.

"Are you okay?" Freddie said.

"I've decided I don't like finding dead bodies," Tree said.

"I tried to reach you on your cell phone," Freddie said. Her eyes searched his.

"I forgot to take it with me."

"The thing is, it's not over yet."

"What do you mean?"

"Come inside."

She led him through the house. Everything became blurred. Only Freddie held focus. Ambient sounds faded. They came out on the terrace. Elizabeth Traven in dark linen slacks and a scoop-necked black top was sitting in a chair close to the pool. She sat up straight, as though about to have her picture taken. Or give testimony.

16

Elizabeth said, "I didn't know where else to go."

"The police are looking for you," was all Tree could say.

"I thought this would be the one place they wouldn't look. At least, not immediately."

"So you know what's happened."

"Yes, of course."

"What do you mean, 'of course.'" Tree's voice rose in unexpected anger. "There is no 'of course' about it. I know your husband is dead because I was there."

"So was I," Elizabeth said quietly.

"You set me up," Tree said. "You stabbed him with a pair of scissors and then you called me, made it sound as though you were in trouble so I would go over there—and what? Provide you with some sort of crazy alibi?"

"I didn't kill Brand," Elizabeth said in a preternaturally calm voice, as though she denied killing her husband every day. "I came into the house, found him on the sofa and called you."

"He was dead?" Tree asked.

"He wasn't moving, there was blood everywhere, so I presumed he was dead."

"Then what did you do?"

"I thought I heard something—someone in the house. I panicked and ran out of the house, drove away. Eventually, I came here."

"I don't understand," Freddie said. "Your husband was hurt. You could see that. Why would you run?"

"As I said, I panicked."

"Why didn't you call the police?" Tree said.

"I don't know. I was scared, I suppose. You think you know how you will react in these situations, but in fact you don't know. You act much differently than you ever imagined."

Freddie stared at her. Elizabeth gave her a steady gaze right back. None of what she was saying sounded very convincing, Tree thought.

"I saw someone running away from the house," Tree said.

"The killer no doubt," Elizabeth said.

"It wasn't you?"

"I told you, I drove away."

"So you didn't kill your husband?"

She made one of her typically dismissive gestures. "I thought he was going to kill me."

"You also said you thought he was having an affair. None of what you tell me turns out to be true. Why should I believe you now?"

"Because I am going to go to the police in a few minutes and undoubtedly they will accuse me of my husband's murder and probably arrest me, so I'm going to require your continued services, Mr. Callister, in order to prove my innocence."

"I'm not so sure you're innocent."

"Good," Elizabeth said. "If you can be convinced I didn't do this terrible thing, then maybe I can convince others as well."

"Who would have wanted to kill him?"

Tree never got the answer to that question because at that moment, someone kicked in the front door. The next thing, heavily-armed men in helmets and flak jackets and armadillo-like armor—science fiction samurai—burst onto the terrace, screaming orders: "Down! Get down. Down!"

Two armored samurai pushed Tree to his knees and then knocked him forward onto the pool deck. Other samurai screamed unintelligible commands, a cacophony of contradictory sounds drowning each other out.

Tree's arms were yanked behind his back, handcuffs snapped around his wrists. He strained for a glimpse of Freddie, also face down on the deck, also being handcuffed. Then Owen Markfield entered his line of vision.

He smiled and said, "You really are as dumb as Cee Jay says you are. Did you think I believed one word out of your mouth?"

17

They didn't hold Freddie long.

However, Elizabeth Traven and Tree were held overnight in the Lee County Justice Center at 1700 Monroe St., downtown Fort Myers. It was Tree's first time in jail. The places you go when you're a private detective, he reflected.

Throughout the night he had a great deal of time to think. He should have been able to come up with something, a clue, a plan, something. But there was nothing. A night in jail only made him more anxious and fearful.

The next morning Tree was finger printed and photographed before being brought in chains to one of the courtrooms in the justice building. From the prisoners' box, Tree could see a pale, grim-faced Freddie seated in a public gallery otherwise filled with reporters present to cover the widow of an international media mogul charged with killing her husband.

Chris was not with Freddie. Tree tried not to be disappointed. Just because a boy's father was in jail, no reason for him to show up.

A few minutes later, Elizabeth Traven, clad in a form-less prison smock that otherwise she would not have been seen dead in, was formally indicted for the murder of her husband. Bail was denied. She was represented by a Fort Myers attorney named T. Emmett Hawkins. With his wispy white hair, navy bow tie, and his beautifully cadenced drawl, Hawkins must have been sent by central casting when the call came for a typical Southern lawyer.

Tree was charged as an accessory to the murder as well as harboring a fugitive. What did they think? That he and Elizabeth had conspired to kill her husband?

The assistant district attorney, a stern young man named Lee Bixby, argued Tree should not be released on bail. Edith Goldman, the no-nonsense defense lawyer Freddie had managed to get hold of first thing that morning, convinced the judge that Tree was neither a flight risk nor a danger to the community. He was released on a twen-ty-five thousand dollar bond, which Freddie put up.

"You're an expensive date," she commented later.

"But worth it?"

Freddie didn't say anything.

By the time Tree was released later that afternoon, most of the reporters and cameramen were gone. A ner-vous young reporter from one of the local stations tried to interview him as he and Freddie strode away from the Justice Center, but he was easily eluded. Tree by now was a minor part of the story; much more interesting was the cable TV talking heads debate as to Elizabeth Traven's in-nocence or guilt.

They crossed the street to the old county courthouse. One imagined the likes of Atticus Finch holding forth elo-quently here; good men bringing justice to the South. A northern view, Tree decided. He and Freddie sat on the courthouse steps.

He expected Freddie to give him hell for getting them into another mess. He said, "I wouldn't blame you if you decide to give me hell for getting us into this mess."

"I'm tempted, believe me," she said. "However, that's probably a waste of breath. Besides, it's not how we got into the mess that counts, it's how we get out. That's why we have Edith."

Who chose that moment to stroll across the park to the courthouse, a slim, elegantly tailored woman with coiffed blond hair, reminding Tree of a middle-aged Lana Turner. Lawyers in bow ties; Lana Turner look-alikes outside ancient courthouses. He was in a 1950s Ross Hunter melodrama. Rock Hudson could have portrayed the romantic fool of a reporter framed by corrupt Southern cops.

"Sorry," Edith said, coming to a stop at the bottom of the steps. "The assistant district attorney, Mr. Lee Bixby, as he usually does, kept me cooling my ridiculously expensive heels."

Tree and Freddie stood up to meet her. "What did he have to say?" Tree said.

"Young Mr. Bixby appears determined to nail your ass," Edith said.

"But Tree had nothing to do with Elizabeth Traven coming to our place," Freddie said. "He was still with the police when she showed up at the door."

"Depending on where this goes, we just may have to convince a jury of that," Edith said. "Here is what they are arguing, and you might as well hear this, too, Freddie. They are saying Tree and Mrs. Traven were having an affair and conspired together to murder Brand Traven."

"You can't be serious," Tree said.

"I don't have to be, because they are," Edith said. "Or they claim they are—which is the same thing."

Tree looked at Freddie. "You know this isn't true."

"Of course I do," Freddie said.

"She's a client, that's all."

"Look," Edith interjected, "no matter what the truth of their allegations, the fact is they don't really want you, Tree."

"They've got a funny way of showing it."

"What they want is your co-operation in their investigation. They want you to tell them something they don't already know."

"But I don't know anything."

"Apparently you do. They want you to implicate Mrs. Traven. Until you co-operate with them, you will remain charged with a very serious crime."

They were interrupted by the arrival of T. Emmett Hawkins. He shook Tree's hand and nodded at Edith. "Sorry to interrupt, Edith, but I wanted to have a quick word with your client."

Edith looked at Tree who shrugged. "It's okay, Edith."

"No, it's not okay, Tree. He is going to want you to agree to things you should not be agreeing to, if you want to avoid going to jail."

"Now, Edith." Hawkins drawl had become particularly honey-soaked. "Mr. Callister is a big boy. He's not going to agree to anything he damned well doesn't want to."

Edith glared.

Hawkins guided Tree over to a small park dominated by an old banyan tree, its roots gnarled and twisted into a thick trunk. Hawkins stopped and inhaled deeply as he took in his surroundings. "It really is lovely, isn't it? A little bit of the past. You know the county was named in 1887 for Robert E. Lee?"

"The South will rise again," Tree said.

"Providing you believe it ever fell in the first place, and more than a few folks around here would argue that notion."

Hawkins leaned forward so that Tree could see the smooth crown of his head overlaid with wisps of white hair. He lowered his voice and that had the effect of thickening his accent even more.

"I've just been speaking with Mrs. Traven. She asked me to remind you that nothing has changed. She still wishes to retain you."

"She does, does she?"

"You can co-ordinate your activities through me, Mr. Callister. I'll report back to Mrs. Traven."

"Do you think this is a good idea? After all, I am charged myself."

"Mrs. Traven is a woman who knows what she wants and doesn't entertain much in the way of alternative suggestions. For good or ill, Mr. Callister, she wants you."

"I'm not sure what I can do for her."

"You can prove her innocence."

"Me?" Tree didn't mean to sound quite so surprised.

Emmett Hawkins blinked a couple of times before he said, "It's the bow tie."

"What about it?"

"It makes people believe I'm more flamboyant and therefore more successful than I am. But I'm not, you see. I'm merely a local criminal defense lawyer. My offices are around the corner. I should probably say office. Mostly, I rely on public defender cases. If I am to believe Mrs. Traven, she is broke. There's no money for investigators. You're it."

Tree allowed the words to sink in. "Supposing she's guilty?"

"What difference does that make?"

"It might interfere with proving her innocence," Tree said.

"Mrs. Traven has faith in you," Emmett Hawkins said.

Great, Tree thought.

18

Freddie drove Tree to the police compound where they had towed his car. "What did Mr. Hawkins want?"

"He wanted to make certain I was on side," Tree said.

"On side with what?" Freddie asked.

"With the idea that Elizabeth Traven didn't kill her husband."

"But she did kill her husband, didn't she?"

"You heard her. She says she didn't."

"And you believe her?"

"You don't?"

"I can't believe you think she's innocent."

"What was Elizabeth like when she arrived at our place?"

"Calm," Freddie said. "Ridiculously calm, now that I think about it. She said she had to see you. When I told her you had gone over to her house thinking she was in trouble, she just nodded and said she would wait for you to return."

"She didn't say anything about Brand?"

"Not a thing. I asked her if she was in trouble. She said she would like to sit out by the pool. She asked for some water, but otherwise, she sat out there, staring into space."

"I don't know what to believe," Tree said.

"So you're going to help her?"

"I don't know that I can."

"Edith is right, Tree. You could go to jail over this."

"All the more reason to help her," Tree said. "If she doesn't go to jail, I can't go to jail."

When they reached the compound, she kissed him and said she had to get to work.

"Thanks," he said.

"For what?"

"Among other things, believing me."

"And what is it that I believe?"

"That I was not having an affair with Elizabeth Traven. I did not help her kill her husband."

She looked at him.

"You do believe me?"

"Whatever you do, don't go on the lam. Otherwise, I lose twenty-five thousand dollars."

"Is that what they call it?"

"Or have I watched too many old Warner Bros. movies?"

"You can never watch too many old Warner Bros. movies," he said. "And you didn't answer my question."

"Yes," she said. "I believe you."

Freddie did sound as though she meant it.

Didn't she?

"Incidentally," she continued, "in all the excitement, I forget to tell you that neither Chris nor Kendra came home last night."

"They're probably there now," he said. "Wondering what happened."

But they weren't at the house when Tree arrived back. He tried Chris's cell. No answer. There was nothing on the house phone voice mail except reporters asking Tree to call.

He took a long shower and then tried Chris's cell again. Still no answer. Restless, he decided to walk over to the Keylime Bistro and get something to eat.

News of the murder and Tree Callister's role in it, had failed to reach the neighborhood. No one gave him a second glance as he seated himself at an outside table shaded by the thatched roof of the restaurant's bandstand. A youthful waitress gave him a guileless smile and the menu. He ordered coffee. Then he sat back, closing his eyes, inhaling the warm air, trying to push the events of the last twenty-four hours into the background.

He opened his eyes as two men seated themselves at the table. They had round, pale faces that went nicely with their pink, hairless domes. Two bald brothers under the Florida sun.

One of the bald brothers wore glasses. He smiled broadly when he said: "You don't mind if we join you, do you?"

The waitress returned with Tree's coffee. "Have you decided what you would like to order?"

"Not yet," Tree said.

"Don't let us interrupt you," the larger bald brother said. Bear-like, he could have been a character created for a Pixar animated feature—except not nearly so cute.

"Yeah, please," said the brother with glasses. "Go ahead and order."

The waitress turned her smile on the two interlopers. "Can I bring you gentlemen menus?"

"No we're fine," the bear-like guy said.

"I'll just stick with the coffee for now," Tree said, abruptly not hungry any more.

"Well, if you change your mind..." The waitress widened her grin and hurried away.

The brother with the glasses leaned forward as though to get a better look. "Maybe you can help us with a little argument we're having."

"I'm sorry," Tree said. "What's this all about? Who are you?"

"My friend here buys into the traditional government-sponsored line, you know, that NASA landed Neil Armstrong on the moon in 1969."

"Which is what happened," the big bald guy without glasses said peevishly. "You would be out of your mind to believe anything else. All this conspiracy stuff is nonsense."

"Not so fast, Elmer," the guy with the glasses said. "There is reliable evidence that in fact the Americans did not land on the moon. That in order to beat the Russians, NASA, with the help of the British filmmaker Stanley Kubrick, conspired to make it *look* as though there was a moon landing, when in fact it never happened."

"This is so utterly ridiculous, Fudd," Elmer-without-the-glasses said. "It's not worth the breath it takes to argue the point. Why would Kubrick ever allow himself to get involved in such a hare-brained conspiracy?"

"Because the government agreed to provide him with the unlimited ability to make movies without ever leaving his estate in England," Fudd said. "If you look at the facts, Elmer, which of course you refuse to do, you would see that after 1969 Kubrick never left England and never again made a studio movie. Where did his financing come from at a time when every other director in the world was scrambling for money? Let's face it, the guy was no Steven

Spielberg when it came to box office hits. The money had to come from NASA."

"In return for some unused footage from *2001: A Space Odyessy*? I don't believe it."

"It wasn't just the unused footage, although they did incorporate some of it," maintained Fudd. "He actually filmed the faked moon landing. We have his widow's sworn testimony. Kubrick also oversaw filming of the so-called astronauts on subsequent moon 'landings.'"

"Elmer and Fudd," Tree said. "You guys are Elmer and Fudd?"

The two men looked at him blankly. "What's wrong with that?" said Fudd.

"Come on. What's going on here? What's the joke?"

Fudd turned his head so that the light glinted off his glasses, making him somehow more ominous. "What makes you think this is a joke, Tree? You're not one of those suckers who has been duped into believing we actually landed on the moon. Are you?"

"How do you know my name?"

Fudd said, "Maybe we've been watching the local TV news this morning, Tree. Maybe we know all about you and the trouble you are in."

"Or it could be," interjected bear-like Elmer, "that it goes beyond that."

Fudd looked vaguely irritated. "Goes beyond *that*? How could it 'go beyond *that*?' What's *that* supposed to mean?"

"It could mean we knew about Tree even before all the stuff on the news," Elmer said.

"Okay. I see your point." Fudd nodded eagerly. "Yes, of course. Maybe we did know all about Tree, the former Chicago newspaperman, tossed out of the profession he loved after many years of loyal service. Tree, who then retreated to Sanibel Island with his lovely wife, Freddie, to become, what? What is it you became down here, Tree?"

"What do you guys want?" Tree said.

"Fudd, you know very well that Tree turned himself into a private detective, a life-changing decision if there ever was one—albeit a pretty stupid decision, if you ask me."

"Hold on there, hoss," Fudd said. "That's a trifle unfair, don't you think?"

Elmer said, "Think about it. A sixty-year-old guy decides to become a detective. He knows nothing about it, has no experience. What sort of moron does that? He leaves himself vulnerable to exactly the sort of trouble he now finds himself in."

Fudd bobbed his bald head up and down. "I see your point, yes I do. Tree was indicted on very serious charges this morning. He's got bigger problems to deal with, so perhaps we should get to the point of our visit."

Elmer trained his eyes on Tree. "I apologize to you, sir. Of course we should get to why we are here, so we can get the problem resolved as quickly as possible."

"Resolve what?" Tree was growing impatient.

"The issue of Kendra and her husband, Chris."

Now that really did catch Tree by surprise. "What about them? What issue?"

Fudd had been rocking back in his chair. Now he stopped. "We represent a client persuaded by your son and his wife to invest in their Chicago enterprise."

"An online dating service," said Elmer in a knowledgeable voice.

"I believe that's what it was," said Fudd. "In due course, Kendra made certain promises to my client, promises she failed to keep. Not only was my client cheated out of a great deal of money, but he feels personally betrayed by Kendra Callister."

"He seeks redress," Elmer said.

"Redress," Fudd repeated. "I'm not sure that's the right word."

Elmer turned his big head toward his partner and unleashed a cold-eyed glower. "Redress most certainly is the right word. He wants his money back. *Redress.*"

"All right, fine. Have it your way." Fudd heaved a sigh and looked over at Tree as though to say: *You see what I'm up against.* "Redress it is. He wants redress."

"Redress for what?" Tree said.

Both men looked vaguely surprised. Elmer spoke: "He wants her back, of course."

"Wants who back?"

"Who?" said Elmer. "Who does everyone lust after in this convoluted little scenario? Well, not the two of us, of course. We are beyond lust where she is concerned. But no one else appears mature enough to see her for what she is and keep their hands off her."

"You're talking about Kendra," Tree said.

"Bingo," said Fudd.

"But who wants her back?"

"Our client," said Elmer.

"Who is your client?"

"Ask your daughter-in-law," Elmer said.

It was Fudd's turn to deliver a laser-like scowl. "I told you not to say that," he snarled. "I made it clear that I didn't want you saying that."

"Why not? What's he gonna do? *Not* ask Kendra. How ridiculous is that? We say to him our client wants Kendra back, but we won't say who the client is. Does it not stand to reason he would ask her?"

"I told you not to say that," Fudd repeated.

"Maybe you should stop giving me so many orders," Elmer said. "Maybe you bark so many orders, it all starts to get confusing, and I forget things."

They were interrupted by the reappearance of the waitress. She looked unhappily at the coffee and then addressed Tree. "Is your coffee all right, sir?"

"It's fine," Tree said.

"It's just that you don't seem to have touched it."

"It's fine."

She looked at Elmer and Fudd. "Sure I can't bring you gentlemen anything?"

"You're very kind," said Fudd with a shake of his head.

The waitress, looking uneasy, wandered off.

"Anyhow," Fudd said, "that's where we are, Tree. That's what brings us to this lovely island."

"Our first visit," added Elmer.

"But hopefully not our last," Fudd said.

"You guys seem to be threatening me," Tree said

"I wouldn't put it that way," said Fudd. "We're not there yet. At the threats, I mean. We're approaching you today, Tree, because you seem to be a sane, reasonable adult, and we need to enlist your help with two young people who are not behaving responsibly."

"I'm not sure what Kendra promised your client," Tree said.

"I thought that was clear enough, Tree," said Fudd in an annoyed voice. "She promised to *be* with him. He would invest in the business, and she would go off into the sunset with him. Not that I can imagine either Kendra or my client walking into any sunsets, but nonetheless, that's the promise that was made."

"Why don't we say forty-eight hours?" Elmer said.

"Forty-eight hours for what?" Tree demanded.

"It's the time we're giving you to deliver Kendra to us and produce some sort of repayment plan for my client."

"Repayment plan? What kind of repayment plan?"

"A repayment plan that retires a five hundred thousand dollar loan," Fudd said.

"They *owe* five hundred thousand dollars?" Tree said in astonishment.

"Lot of money, isn't it?" Elmer said. "More than a private detective earns these days, I'm willing to bet. But that is how much our client is willing to settle for."

"That's impossible," Tree said.

"Tree, I don't know you very well so I hate to make snap judgment calls," Fudd said. "But what kind of parent were you, to allow your son to grow up so stupid?"

"Chris isn't stupid." The assertion sounded lame, even to Tree's ears.

"Anyone who gets himself mixed up with a woman like Kendra and then pisses off our client, you've got to wonder if he was properly raised."

"Believe me, Tree," Elmer said, nodding at his companion, "we both know something about the lack of proper parenting."

"My mother was a wonderful person," Fudd said.

"She just liked a bottle of vodka before noon," Elmer said.

"I'm not going to get into petty arguments about my mother," Fudd said.

"I'm not even talking about the afternoon vodka bottle," Elmer said.

Fudd produced a wallet. "Here let me pay for your coffee, Tree."

"Then there was the bottle or two of merlot with dinner. Lovely woman."

Fudd gritted his teeth and put a ten dollar bill on the table. "Now the thing is Tree, we may not look very threatening, but believe me, we are."

"Just ask Kendra," Elmer said, standing.

Tree managed to say, "How do I get in touch with you?"

Oh, that's all right," Fudd said, pushing his chair back and following Elmer to his feet. "We'll be in touch with you."

"Wait a minute," Elmer said.

Fudd once again looked irritated. "What is it now? We're going to miss our tour boat."

"He never said."

"Said what?"

"Which side of the argument he favors."

Fudd looked at Tree. "What do you think, Tree? Did Stanley Kubrick help NASA fake the moon landing? He did, didn't he?"

Tree stared at them.

19

Tree sat behind the wheel of the Beetle in the parking lot below the main entrance to the Lani Kai Island Resort, taking deep breaths, trying to calm himself, wondering how much stress it would take to induce a heart attack in a man his age.

He had discovered a rich man with a pair of scissors in his throat. He had spent a night in jail before being charged with helping his client kill her husband—not to mention being accused of sleeping with her. Two threatening strangers with the unlikely names of Fudd and Elmer were after his son and daughter-in-law, both of whom had disappeared.

And, oh yes, he was supposed to prove innocent the client who probably had killed her husband.

That should be more than enough stress to induce the killing heart attack. For the moment, however, he decided to concentrate on the Traven passenger. Why would Brand Traven have driven all the way up to Coleman to pick him up? A few hours later Traven was dead. Could the man he retrieved from Coleman have killed him? Or was Elizabeth right and her husband was trying to kill her, and the Traven passenger was the man who was supposed to do it?

He got out of the car and went up the steps, past the mural featuring the dancing native girls and down the walkway to the staircase that led him up to the lobby. A young woman with glasses wearing a short-sleeved white shirt stood behind the counter. A name tag that said, "Jenny" was pinned to the front of her blouse. Jenny had been the desk clerk on duty when he was here before.

"How may I help you?" She did not sound very interested in helping anyone.

Tree explained that he was a private detective. Jenny adjusted her glasses to get a better look and then grinned, showing front teeth the size of tombstones. "Come on, you're not really a private detective, are you? I mean, where's your trench coat?"

"A lot of people ask me that," Tree said amiably. "I always tell them it's too hot down here for trench coats. Soon as it cools off, that's when I wear one."

Jenny stopped smiling. Her eyes narrowed suspiciously. "How do I know you're a private detective?"

Tree pulled out his wallet and showed her his Florida license, complete with his photo.

"The State of Florida gave you that?"

"They didn't give it to me; they sold it to me after I completed the course."

"You can take a course to be a private detective?"

"You bet."

Jenny's eyes narrowed further. "Aren't you a little old to be a private detective?"

Tree tried hard to keep his grin in place. "How old do you have to be?"

"You know, for the rough stuff."

"There's not ordinarily a lot of rough stuff," Tree said. "Right now, for example, I'm just looking into the whereabouts of a person."

"Oh, yeah? What kind of person?"

"An African American. Mid-thirties. He checked in about four o'clock yesterday afternoon."

"No African American checked in here at four o'clock or any other time yesterday. We had some folks around noon. A husband and wife down from Canada. But that was it."

"No one else checked in?"

"Checked in? No."

"Jenny, a heavyset black man in his thirties did come in here about four o'clock yesterday."

"How do you know that?"

"Because I was here. I saw him."

Her face had gone flat.

"He was standing right here at the desk, talking to you."

"Okay, that guy," she said in a subdued voice. "He didn't check in. So I wasn't lying."

"Any idea why he didn't?"

She shrugged. "He asked about the room rates. Then he asked if he could leave his bag here for a few minutes while he went downstairs for a beer. He came back half an hour later, said he'd changed his mind, picked up his bag, and left."

"Did you tell the police this?"

"The police?" Jenny looked worried. "The police haven't been here."

"Okay, Jenny, thanks. I appreciate your help."

"Next time, wear a trench coat," Jenny said.

If Traven's passenger did not check into this hotel, then where did he go? Tree wondered as he stood on the Lani Kai's portico and leaned against the railing, gazing out at Estero Boulevard.

Tree walked along Estero checking the small tourist hotels and motels. They yielded nothing.

Toward the western end of the boulevard, he came to the Gulf Motel, a gray-painted frame structure with screen doors and a sign propped against the latticework foundation announcing in bright red letters: "Cool Pool." Who could resist?

Tree entered the office. A large woman stood behind the reception desk. She wore a sleeveless print blouse that showed off an intricately scaled dragon crawling up her left arm. She said, "Tree Callister."

He looked at her. The woman said, "You don't remember me?"

The dragon tattoos. Of course. "Molly Lightower," he said. "The Dragon Lady."

She grinned and said, "I helped you out with your detecting a while back over at Fennimore's Cycle Shop."

"So you did, Molly, and I appreciate it. What brings you here?"

A look of sadness crossed her face. "Me and my man had a bit of a falling out. Figured it was best to take what they call in these confusing times, a time-out."

"I thought you said he tamed a Hells Angels mama."

"Well, he did at that," she conceded. "Trouble is Russ failed to tame his urges with other mamas."

"Sorry to hear that, Molly. You deserve better."

"That's what I told Russ. We need to be true to one another. If we aren't true, what's the point?"

"I agree," Tree said.

She gave him a sad smile. "He likes them fat and stupid. I'm fat enough, but I guess I just don't fill the stupid part very well."

"I'm sorry, Molly."

"What can you do? Life sucks, sometimes. But we go on. Not like there's a whole lot of choice. So here I am watching over this place for my girlfriend, Shirley. She's up in Tallahassee romancing her new fella. Well, good for her. Meanwhile, Mr. Tree Callister, what can I do you for? You need more help with your detecting?"

"You didn't happen to work yesterday did you?"

"I'm working every day and night while Shirley's in love in Tallahassee."

"I'm looking for an African American male who may have checked in here sometime after four o'clock."

"Sure, I remember. Big dude. A jailhouse rat."

"How did do you know he was in prison?"

"Are you kidding? I grew up around punks like him. Bad guys. You can smell them as soon as they walk in the room."

"He checked in?"

"Yeah, but not in the afternoon. About ten o'clock last night. He left this morning."

"You sure it was ten?"

"Absolutely. I was just thinking that was going to be it for the night. The place wasn't going to be even half full. I looked at my watch and then this dude walked in."

"What was his name, Molly?"

"I'm not supposed to do this." Molly found a pair of glasses and put them on. "But seeing as how you and I go back a ways in the detecting business ..."

She stepped over to the computer and pounded thick fingers against a worn keyboard. "Let me see what we got here." She thumped the keyboard some more. "Here he is. Tony Dodge. Paid cash in advance."

"You didn't get a home address?"

"Fort Myers was all he wrote. As long as they pay up, I'm told not to ask questions."

"Have they cleaned his room yet?" Tree asked.

She rolled her eyes. "Things do move around here. But fast is not the word you would use in connection with those things."

"Mind if I take a look in there?"

She studied him a beat and then shrugged. "Potential customer comes in, wants to see a room before he rents it. Who can blame him?" She dropped a key on the counter. "Number three at the other end."

"Thanks, Molly. Won't take long." He picked the key up.

"No hurry. By the time anyone gets around to cleaning that room, hell, Russ could have discovered how much he misses me, and begged me to come home."

"I'm willing to bet that's going to happen," Tree said.

Molly gave a winsome smile. "Better stick to detecting, Tree."

Tree didn't need the key as it turned out. The inside door to number three was wide open. He opened the screen and stepped into the room.

The queen-size bed was unmade. That and the wet towels strewn across the carpet were the only outward signs anyone had occupied the room.

A smear of shaving cream lingered in the bathroom sink. A puddle of water glistened on the tile floor beside a soggy bathmat. A face cloth dripped off the side of the bathtub. Tree picked up the waste basket that stood beside the toilet. He poked at a couple of used tissues and a torn envelope. He picked out the envelope and replaced the waste basket on the floor. Dodge had used a pencil to print a single word on the envelope in capital letters:

SASHA

Beneath it was an address: 144 Acacia Rd.

———

Tree left the motel and walked back to where he had parked his car at the Lani Kai. He got inside and phoned Freddie at work. To his surprise, she picked up after the first ring. "Are you near a computer?"

"Happen to be sitting right beside one," she said.

"Do me a favor, will you? Go to Google maps and see what you get when you type in 144 Acacia Rd."

"You need an iPad," she said.

"Do I?"

"That way you wouldn't have to call me. Where are you, anyway?"

"I'm outside the Lani Kai on Estero Boulevard."

"What are you doing there?"

"Following a lead." Did he sound like a detective? Freddie snorted.

Maybe not.

"Have you found anything?" Tree said.

"Let me see. There is an Acacia Road in Sarasota."

"Nothing around here?"

"Sarasota is all I can see."

"Okay. Thanks, Freddie. One more thing. Ray owns a place in Naples, doesn't he?"

"My Ray? Ray Dayton?"

"The Ray Man. I thought he said something a while ago about a house in Naples."

Freddie said carefully, "It was his mother's."

"Do you know the address?"

"Tree." Her voice now contained a warning note. "What are you up to?"

"Following a couple of hunches, that's all."

"Okay, but one of those hunches should not involve Ray Dayton. I have to work with this man."

"It's probably nothing. Just humor me, please."

"There is a line of thought that argues I humor you too much."

"You can't possibly believe that," he said. "Do you have the address?"

"Don't get yourself into more trouble with Ray, okay?"

"Perish the thought."

"The address I have in Naples is 345 Old Wildway Rd. He's been trying to sell it."

"Thanks."

"You don't want to tell me what's going on?"

"I'm going to drive up to Sarasota. Check a couple of things out."

"On Acacia Road?"

"It's probably a wild goose chase."

"Just remember, Tree, you're out on bail. If you have another run-in with the police, they revoke that bail. Not only am I out twenty-five thousand dollars, but you'll be cooling your heels in a jail cell."

"I'm not going to get into trouble. Promise."

"The last time you said that, you got shot."

"An anomaly."

"I'm not certain that's the correct use of that word, but I'll let it go for now."

"I love you," he said.

"Don't get yourself killed."

Right, he thought to himself. He shouldn't do that.

20

One hundred forty-four Acacia Rd. was a strip mall on the outskirts of Sarasota, a series of desolate two-story buildings surrounding a deserted parking lot. There were too many similar malls throughout the state.

Tree parked and walked over to the main entrance. On one side of the double glass doors was a Walgreen Pharmacy. On the other side was a discount furniture store with a "For Lease" sign, faded with age, propped in one of its dust-streaked windows.

Tree stepped into a linoleum-floored lobby blasted by cold air from an unseen air conditioner. An elevator stood to the left of a set of stairs. Next to the stairs was a building directory listing companies with names like, "SAR SO A INVESTME S LTD."

He studied the directory, baffled. Why would Tony Dodge want to come here?

A skinny guy with jet black hair bounced down the stairs. He wore a black suit. He stopped to give Tree the once-over. Tree stared back. In a Spanish-accented rasp, the skinny guy said, "Who you looking for?"

Tree said, "I'm looking for Sasha."

The guy said, "I'm Sasha."

What to say to that?

"They said to come in here and ask for you."

"I thought we were gonna be short a guy tonight," Sasha said.

"No, no," Tree said.

"Okay, well listen, amigo, you're late."

"Sorry," Tree said. "I had trouble finding this place."

"Yeah, yeah," Sasha said impatiently. "Don't sweat it. Follow me."

He turned and went back up the stairs, taking two at a time. Tree hurried to keep up with him. When they reached the second floor, they went along the hall to a door with a sign that said "RED ROSE." All the letters were neatly in place.

"Is this the outfit I'm working for?" Tree asked, indicating the sign.

Sasha fished around in his pocket, came up with a set of keys. "You're working for me, amigo, and that's all you know."

He chose a key, and used it to unlock the door. "Come on," he said. "We're gonna be late."

He pressed a wall plate illuminating an office containing a desk and a chair. A wardrobe stretched the length of the room. Sasha opened the doors to reveal a rack of black suits. Peaked caps filled the shelf above the suit racks. Sasha flipped through the suits. "What size are you? Take a look through here, find something that fits."

As Tree approached the wardrobe, Sasha went over to the desk, opened a bottom drawer and began pulling out white shirts, folded and wrapped in plastic. "One of these should fit," he said. In another drawer Sasha found a black tie and threw it on top of the shirt. "Get changed and then meet me downstairs as soon as you can. Chop, Chop."

"Sure," Tree said.

"Also get one of the caps. See you in a minute." Sasha dashed out the door, closing it behind him.

Mystified as to what this was all about, Tree nonetheless went through the rack until he found a suit that looked to be the right size. He stripped off his clothes and climbed into the trousers. Not bad. Then he chose a shirt with his neck size, tore off the plastic wrapping, and put it on. The collar was tight but it would be fine.

He adjusted one of the caps so that the peak hung low over his eyes. He gathered up his own clothes and went down to the lobby. No Sasha. Tree stood there, holding his clothes, wondering what to do. Then Sasha burst through the entrance door, out of breath. "All set?"

"What do I do with my clothes?"

"Stick them in your car on the way over. Come on. Chop. Chop."

He turned and pushed through the glass doors. Tree went after him. Outside, hit by a wall of late afternoon heat, he deposited his clothes in the Beetle and then followed Sasha to another parking area behind the mall. Six white limousines were lined up beside each other. Party limos, Tree thought, so where was the party? Five men huddled near the limos, all dressed similarly to Tree. They looked around expectantly as Sasha and Tree advanced.

"Okay, everybody, listen up." The five men broke ranks and came over to Sasha. One of the men dropped his cigarette to the pavement and then used his heel to grind it out.

Sasha pointed to a small, dark-complexioned man. "Tango here, he's gonna take the lead car. You others follow him. He'll take you over to the house. You don't speak

unless you're spoken to. Got that?" When everyone nodded, Sasha said, "Okay, let's get going. Chop. Chop. Take
it slow and easy. I'll give you further instructions later. Any
questions? Good."

The others headed for their assigned limos. Sasha mo-
tioned to Tree and then jerked his thumb at the last limo in
the line. "Keys in the ignition. Chop, chop."

Tree, heart beating ridiculously fast, double-timed over
to the limo and opened the driver's side door. Immediately, he was hit by the scent of perfume and a blast of
rap music. The music emanated from the car's stereo. The
perfume came from the four young women seated in the
softly lit vastness of the car's interior.

21

The four women could not have been any more than eighteen or nineteen. Not beauties exactly but impeccably creamed and blushed and rouged, dripping with glittery jewelry and dressed to kill in short tight skirts. They chattered excitedly in Spanish.

Tree said, "Hey, there, ladies."

Nobody paid any attention. He was the help. They were the stars. He finally caught the eye of a reed-thin Latina with violet Elizabeth Taylor eyes and jet black hair falling in thick waves.

He said to her, "Any idea what this is all about?"

She shrugged. "Some rich guy."

"Party time," the only blond member of the quartet added with a bright smile.

"Do you know who the rich guy is?"

The Latina kid shrugged. "Axe. X. Something like that."

A plump African American woman said, "Aksel Baldur. That's the dude's name. I Googled him. Makes cheap

clothes or something. Big deal. He's rich. That's all you
have to know."

"Maybe I'll marry him," said Elizabeth Taylor eyes.

"You stand in line, baby," the blonde said.

Everyone giggled. "Hey, dude, quit talking and get this
hearse rolling," said the Latina.

A chorus of agreement rose from the back. Tree waved
a hand in surrender, straightened around, found the key in
the ignition and started the engine. The excited Spanish
chatter resumed.

The limo ahead of him started forward. Tree slid the
gear shift into drive and the car lurched ahead. That's when
it struck him that he had never driven anything this size
before. Anywhere near this size, come to think of it.

As it turned out, any driving expertise proved unnec-
essary. The limo convoy proceeded along for barely two
miles before the convoy turned through golden gates that
opened onto a sprawling seaside mansion built around and
above clusters of live oaks and banyans so that it resembled
a gigantic tree house; a boy's thirty million dollar dream. Its
vastness silenced the backseat chatter and replaced it with
admiring gasps.

A tiled drive swung beneath a portico where the limos
disgorged their glamorous passengers: dozens of eager,
squealing young women in revealing party dresses.

It was Tree's turn under the portico. Well-muscled
young men bursting out of black Armani suits, outfitted
with plastic earpieces, stood in clusters, taking pride in the
level of menace they could display.

A tall, broad-shouldered man surged out of the mansion as Tree opened the passenger door. Tree recognized
Aksel Baldur from his clothing ads.

Gold chains and medallions glittered against a massive
bronzed chest framed by the white linen shirt open to the

waist. Luxurious frosted blond hair flowed to his shoulders. He would have fit right into a Bee Gees tour, circa 1977.

Tree's passengers tumbled out amid a chorus of shrieks and laughter, gleefully embracing their hugely smiling new best friend.

"Okay, fella, move it along," snarled a security guard. Tree got back in the limo and rolled the car forward, following the road away from the entrance. Sasha on the roadside waved him to a stop. "Take it around to the back," he said. "Chop. Chop."

Tree nodded and spun the limo along the drive. He turned off the stereo. Blessed silence. A parking area lay beyond a low retaining wall. A section had been roped off for more than a dozen limos. Tree parked at the end of the line and turned off the engine. His cell phone buzzed. It was Freddie.

"Just checking to make sure you're still alive," she said.

"I'm in Sarasota," he said.

"What are you doing up there?"

"Driving beautiful women around in a block-long limo."

There was a fair amount of dead air before Freddie said, "I never know whether you're kidding."

"I'm even wearing a chauffeur's outfit."

"I guess my next question is—why are you chauffeuring beautiful young women around?"

"Just part of the job," Tree said.

Sasha rapped on the driver's side window, causing him to jump. "Got to go," he said to Freddie. "I'll call you later."

He closed down his cell phone and got out of the car. "What are you doing?" demanded Sasha.

"I'm on the phone," Tree said.

"Make phone calls on your own time. You're working for me, you pay attention to business. Understand?"

"Sure."

"Come on over with the guys."

The drivers were gathered just beyond the line of parked limos as Sasha and Tree approached.

"Okay, listen up fellas," Sasha said. "Here's the way it goes down for the rest of the night. Chances are we won't be needed, but if we are, they call me and I send one of you around front with a car to pick up passengers. You deliver them where they want to go. Don't know how to get there? That's why there's a GPS installed in each one of these babies."

One of the men asked, "How long we supposed to hang around?"

"You hang around as long as I tell you to hang around. That's what you're getting paid for. I'll be back in a while."

Sasha stalked off. Inside the house, a band struck up its version of "I Can't Get No Satisfaction."

A short guy with a pock-marked face dragged on his cigarette. "I don't get it," he said. "All these available broads. They barely speak English and don't even seem to know where they are."

The guy Sasha called Tango said, "Like the man stated, you drive the car and don't ask questions."

"You ask questions you get into trouble," someone else agreed.

"That Aksel, he likes the babes, for sure," Tango said. "I can't tell you how many chicks I've driven up here— kids. Who knows what kind of shit they get themselves into?"

That produced knowing chuckles from the group.

"Wetbacks," the pock-marked guy said.

"What's that supposed to mean?" Tree said.

"If there's one green card among those babies, I'd like to see it," said the pock-marked guy.

"Never mind the green card," Tango said. "If they were checking IDs, none of these girlies would be old enough to get in the door."

"What can you do?" the pock-marked guy said. "You're rich, you get the pussy. You're poor, you drive the pussy."

Tree heard something behind him and turned as Sasha reappeared. Everyone grew quiet. Sasha pointed at Tree. "You. What'd you say your name was?"

"Bill," Tree said.

"Okay, Bill. Come with me. Chop. Chop."

"What's up?" Tree said.

"You know what, Bill?" Sasha said. "You ask too many questions. Just do as you're told and come with me."

He followed Sasha across the parking lot. They went around the corner of the house. Sasha abruptly veered to the right so Tree could get a better view of Fudd and Elmer coming toward him.

"Hi, Tree," Fudd said.

"You can't imagine what a surprise it was to see you drive up to the front of the house," Elmer said.

He stepped forward raising a fist the size of a ham. He used it to smash Tree in the mouth.

22

Tree dropped to the ground, his mouth filling with the warm taste of blood.

Fudd and Elmer grabbed his arms, half-carried, half-dragged him across an expanse of lawn onto another drive. The gleaming black curve of a Lincoln Towncar came into view. Tree could hear sounds of music and merriment—a pretty good version of "A Whole Lot of Shakin' Goin' On"— rich people having a swell time while the poor were being beaten to death out back.

Fudd and Elmer plopped him down at the rear of the Lincoln. As if by magic, the trunk popped up; the yawning entrance to the rabbit hole. Tree should have screamed, "No, not the trunk." Except his mouth was full of blood, and he couldn't get the words out. Just as well, he thought dimly. The words would sound silly and would have no effect.

Fudd and Elmer lifted him up and without ceremony dropped him into the trunk. He looked up in time to glimpse a blue-black Florida sky splayed with stars before darkness descended, and the beaten old pharaoh was entombed.

Okay, Tree thought, this is what it's like inside an automobile trunk—pitch black with panic roiling the pit of his stomach. A trifle claustrophobic, too, but nothing that a two-fisted private detective like Tree Callister couldn't handle—a detective so tough he could be felled by a single blow, reduced to such a weakened state that a couple of thugs could throw him into a trunk with no more effort than it takes to lift a sack of potatoes.

The Lincoln lurched forward. His head banged against something solid. He fought off an abrupt rise in the level of his claustrophobia. As the car picked up speed, his stomach twisted and dropped, producing the same nausea he experienced as a kid when his parents forced him to sit in the back of their big green Chrysler, the air filled with the smell of stale cigarette smoke. Damn. He shouldn't have thought of that. He must not throw up. Not in these cramped confines.

He tried to think of something else. He thought about Fudd and Elmer who said they represented a client crazy for Kendra Callister. Was Aksel Baldur that client? Was he the rich man so anxious to have Kendra back he would send a couple of hired thugs after her?

It looked that way.

And were those same thugs capable of killing Kendra's father-in-law because he crashed a party?

That appeared to be a possibility.

The car turned a corner. He braced himself by pushing the palms of his hands against the trunk lid. His stomach rumbled and dropped again. Bile filled his throat. He was going to be sick. Then the car lurched to a stop.

Silence, save for the ticking sounds of metal at rest. His stomach continued to churn. The air was close. The trunk flipped open. Hands wrenched him out and dropped him to the ground.

He became aware that the Lincoln had parked at the edge of some sort of junkyard. There was no more time to contemplate his surroundings, however, as either Fudd or Elmer—in the darkness and confusion it was hard to tell—chose that moment to deliver a hard kick to his ribs. He didn't so much gasp—he would have preferred the manly gasp—as howl in pain, certain that the force of the kick had shattered his rib cage.

On the watery edges of his vision, he had the impression of someone bending over him, peering down to get a better look at the damage inflicted.

"Really stupid." Elmer's voice fluttered through the hurt.

"I couldn't agree more," said Fudd, from somewhere off. He delivered the next blow. Tree produced a truly awful howl.

Elmer continued in an all-too-reasonable voice: "You are a stupid amateur, Tree, and too old to boot. You have stumbled into the jungle, and we are the wild animals in the jungle, and you are helpless against us."

"Any doubts about that," Fudd added in an equally reasonable voice, "and you just have to look at the predicament you're in."

"Also, look at your total lack of ability to do anything about it," Elmer said. "Take note of that. It really is pathetic."

"Truly pathetic," Fudd agreed.

Tree heard a dull hard splat, like a baseball bat hitting a water melon. Fudd dropped in front of him, glasses clattering to the pavement, mouth agape.

He looked up to see a massive form hit Elmer in the stomach. He issued a high-pitched shriek and joined Fudd on the ground. The form shifted and the available light revealed Ferne Clowers in jeans and a long-sleeved T-shirt with an upraised baseball bat.

"I don't know who you tom cats are," Ferne said, standing over the prone bodies of Tree's assailants. "But hear this: Tree Callister is a friend of mine. Got it? Hey, there, pal." She nudged Fudd with the tip of her bat. "Got it?"

Fudd managed to move his head up and down.

"So you leave him alone. Okay?" That got a prompt nod from Elmer. "Otherwise, next time I don't bring a bat. I come back with a meat cleaver. That doesn't work, it goes to guns. I got big guns, believe me."

She came over and looked down at Tree, her face shadowed and gentle, a descending angel sent to save him. A *big* angel, but an angel. Not so long ago she was trying to kill him. Tonight, she was saving his life.

He struggled to his knees.

"Let's get out of here," she said.

Not a bad idea, Tree thought, a moment before she yanked him upright. Not a bad idea at all.

23

Whooo-hoooo!" Ferne bellowed as she drove her Cadillac Eldorado back to Fort Myers. "Nothing like it. Nothing like a gal with a baseball bat to focus your attention."

Tree, in pain from his swelling mouth and what he imagined was his shattered rib cage, said, "You didn't kill them, did you?"

"So what if I did, Tree? They were about to take you apart. You think there would have been anything left of you if I hadn't come along?"

"I don't want anyone dead," he said.

"If I wanted them dead, they'd be dead. As it is, I just wanted to mess them up a little so they think about Ferne and her baseball bat every time they take a breath for the next six months or so."

"I think they broke my ribs," Tree said.

"We'll get them taped up," Ferne said, as if she dealt with broken ribs all the time.

Tree settled into the red leather. The pain dispersed a bit. He found he could breathe more easily. "How did you find me?" he asked.

"I didn't find you," she said, keeping her eyes on the road. "I followed you."

"Followed me? Why would you follow me?"

"Because I thought you might be getting yourself into trouble, and you might just need a gal with a baseball bat."

"I don't like the idea of you following me, Ferne."

"I'm sorry, Tree. Why don't I take you back to those two jerks?"

"Don't get me wrong, I appreciate what you did for me."

"Glad to hear it," Ferne said.

"Although I don't quite understand it."

"What's not to understand? I like you. I help the people I like. Everyone else, look out."

"How can you like me, Ferne? A few days ago you were trying to kill me."

"What can I tell you? Us gals are fickle creatures. Besides, you've got enough enemies without adding me to the list. Why were those two after you, anyway?"

"They're working for a guy who wants my daughter-in-law."

Ferne gave him a quick glance. "You gotta be kidding. The guy who owns that mansion?"

"His name's Aksel Baldur."

"Axe-and-bladder? What the hell kind of name is that?"

"He's a Finn, I think."

"A fin? What's a fin?"

"Someone from Finland."

"What's your daughter-in-law doing with a guy from Finland?"

"That's a good question," Tree said.

"And why are you mixed up in it?"

"Another good question," Tree said.

"Because the next time, Tree darling, love you though I do, I might not be around to save your behind."

"Fern, you don't love me."

"From the moment I walked into your office," Ferne said in a serious voice. "I've never experienced anything like it. It was as if I had been hit by lightning or something. I didn't know what to do. I had it all arranged to take you up there to Matlacha and have Slippery finish you off. But I couldn't do it, Tree. When the rubber hit the road, I couldn't bring myself to do it. Weirdest thing."

"But why would you want to kill me in the first place?"

"Because of what you did to a friend of mine."

Tree looked at her, more confused than ever. "What friend? What did I do?"

"Dwayne Crowley. You killed him."

"How did you know Dwayne?"

"We were in Coleman together," Ferne said. "Cellmates. I loved him. He loved me, although, to be honest, Dwayne wasn't always very successful in showing his true feelings."

"But how could the two of you have been in Coleman?"

"This was before I became a woman," Ferne said.

A long beat ensued before Tree managed to say, "Before you became a woman?"

"For a long time, I was a woman trapped in a man's body," Ferne said. "At Coleman I was transformed into my true self. Ferlin Flowers became Ferne Clowers."

"You could do that in prison?"

"Sweetheart, you can do anything in prison."

"What were you in for?"

"Nothing too serious. They said I hijacked some trucks."

"That was it?"

"Okay. And attempted murder."

They drove in silence for a time.

"My cousin Len actually stole the trucks," Ferne added. "I just drove one or two of them across state lines. A bad move on my part."

"Dwayne was coming at me with a shotgun," Tree said. "He'd already killed an FBI agent."

"I imagine Dwayne could be a mean bastard with a shotgun," Ferne said.

"I didn't have a whole lot of choice; it was going to be either him or me. I thought it would be me for certain. No one was more surprised than I was when it turned out to be him."

"Dwayne probably got what he deserved," Ferne said. "In retrospect I can see that. Still, I felt I had to do something, you know, avenge his death. Kill the killer. But as soon as I walked into your office I got this gentle, loving vibe from you. I knew that becoming Ferne had made me a different person, and that I could not kill you. I was in love."

"Except you still drove me up to Matlacha and put me in front of Slippery, who didn't seem to share your love."

"But when he tried to cut you, I stopped him. If that isn't love, I don't know what is."

How could Tree argue with logic like that?

———

By the time Ferne dropped Tree at the Acacia Road mall, it was almost two in the morning. There was no sign of Sasha or young women in tight party dresses. Tree's ribs were hurting and he was dead tired. He was also afraid Ferne might try to kiss him again.

"I don't know how to thank you," he said.

"No thanks necessary," Ferne said. "I'll follow you back to Fort Myers, just in case."

"I appreciate this, Ferne."

"I'm around if you need me. Sort of like your guardian angel."

"Ferne, I don't need a guardian angel."

"Not to argue the point, Tree, but I've never met anyone who needs a guardian angel more than you do. Has anyone ever suggested that you might not be cut out for this line of work?"

"A number of people," Tree said.

"Maybe you should listen to them."

The air in the car felt warm and close. She leaned toward him. He lurched back. "Don't kiss me," he blurted, sounding like a kid on a bad prom night date.

She gave him a sad, hollow smile. "Don't worry, Tree. I'm not going to kiss you. You're a married man, after all."

Now he felt embarrassed. "Listen, Ferne. You've got to be more careful about being around me."

"Why is that?"

"The police are looking for you."

Ferne managed to sound both hurt and angry as she said: "The police have been looking for me my whole life."

She handed him a slip of paper. "What's this?" he asked.

"My telephone number. If you ever want me around, for whatever reason, just give me a call, and I'll be there."

"Thanks, Ferne. I mean it. For everything."

"Get out of the car, Tree. Go home to your wife. And never mind me. I know how to take care of myself. You don't. *You* be careful."

24

Dawn broke over San Carlos Bay as Tree finally reached the causeway leading to the island. Only then did Ferne's headlights disappear from his rear view mirror. He felt a palpable sense of relief when he turned the Beetle into his own driveway on Andy Rosse Lane. He was not so certain he was safe here, but at least he was home.

Hunched and bent against the hurt in his body, he slumped toward the house. Even the act of turning the key in the lock hurt. He opened the door and stepped inside and it was as though someone stuck a red-hot knife in his side. He cried out and the next thing found himself down on all fours. He looked up and saw Freddie standing over him, wearing an oversized T-shirt and a frown.

"What's wrong?" she said.

"What makes you so sure anything's wrong?"

"It's five o'clock in the morning. You're lying on the floor, dressed in what I suppose is your chauffeur's uniform."

"You're very intuitive," Tree said. "Can you help me up?"

"I think so," Freddie said.

"Be careful. I may have broken a couple of ribs."

"Oh, great. How did that happen?"

"A couple of thugs jumped me."

"Tree," she said with a mixture of exasperation and concern. "What are you doing to yourself?"

"You should see the other guys," Tree said.

With Freddie steadying him, he managed to get shakily to his feet. He leaned against her. "You haven't heard from Chris, have you?"

"Not a word. Is this normal behavior? Your son and his wife come for a visit, and then they disappear?"

"I'm not sure normal is a word that applies to Chris and Kendra," Tree said.

"Of course, Chris is a member of a family with a father who comes home at five in the morning with cracked ribs."

"It's a very curious family," Tree agreed. "I tried to warn you."

"I should have listened," Freddie said.

Freddie helped him into the bedroom and sat him on the edge of the bed. She began to strip off his clothes.

"It's a long story," he said.

"It usually is these days," she said.

As briefly as he could, he told her about the two thugs who came looking for Kendra. He told her about following Brand Traven to Coleman where he picked up Tony Dodge, the trip back to Fort Myers Beach, finding the address in the motel waste basket and then ending up in Sarasota behind the wheel of a limo driving young women to Aksel Baldur's oceanfront estate.

"So these thugs work for Aksel Baldur?"

"No question about it."

"And Aksel is the guy who wants Kendra back."

Tree nodded. "It looks like there is something going on involving supplying young women for Baldur's parties."

"Chris and Kendra are part of this?"

"I don't like to think that's what it is," Tree said.

"But it could be."

"Yes."

"Which may account for why they disappeared."

"I'm hoping it isn't," Tree said. "I hope I've got this all wrong."

"What a mess," Freddie said.

Tree moved and winced in pain.

Freddie said, "We should get you to a doctor."

"But then I would have to answer a lot of questions. And right now I don't want to answer any questions. I just want to get some sleep."

"My wounded knight in tarnished armor." The way she said it was not complimentary.

"More like the Cowardly Lion, I'm afraid."

"Good. I'm all for cowardly lions. That way you keep out of trouble and stay alive."

"I love you," he said.

"I know you do."

He waited. Freddie finished getting him undressed. "This is when you're supposed to say, 'I love you, too, darling.'"

She smiled. "I just thought of something."

"You don't love me?"

"Aren't you supposed to be helping Elizabeth Traven prove her innocence?"

"Supposedly, yes."

"How does any of this help her?"

"I'm not sure it does."

"If this Dodge is an ex-con, which, since you picked him up at Coleman, that's what he probably is, then maybe Brand Traven hired him to kill his wife."

Tree looked at her.

"Elizabeth somehow found out about it, and stabbed her husband with the scissors before he could have her killed."

"That's not much of a defense."

"It's better than anything she's got right now."

"Except how do Axel Baldur and the women fit into it—not to mention Chris and Kendra?"

"That's where you come in. You're the detective. You figure it out."

Tree couldn't think any more. He was too tired. He lay on his back getting himself as comfortable as possible while Freddie pulled covers over him.

The last words he heard before drifting into deep sleep were, "Remember, you've got to be in court at ten o'clock this morning."

25

"Why are you walking so funny?" asked Edith Goldman. It was a few minutes after she appeared before Judge Edgar Beckman and got Tree's case put over for another month.

"I hurt my ribs," Tree said.

"How did you do that?"

"Better you don't ask," Tree said.

Edith looked at him as though she already was seeing him in shackles on his way to prison. "You look like hell, if you don't mind my saying so."

"That's because I haven't had much sleep."

"A man your age you should get a proper night's sleep," Edith said.

"A man my age probably shouldn't be standing around the Lee County Justice Center charged with various felonies," Tree said.

"Incidentally, speaking of going to jail, I talked to your friend Lee Bixby, the assistant district attorney, earlier this morning."

"What did he have to say?"

"They are still willing to drop the charges. All they want is some co-operation on the Brand Traven murder."

"They want me to testify against Elizabeth Traven," Tree corrected.

"Okay. Whatever. Why do you have a problem testifying against her?"

"They think I was sleeping with her and then conspired with her to knock off her husband. None of that is true. I can't testify to something that never happened."

Edith responded by stepping closer so that he could not miss her you've-got-a-detention-young-man sternness.

"Mr. Callister, let me put this to you as clearly as I can. The police and the assistant district attorney will have no trouble sending you to jail for a long time unless you co-operate a little more than you are currently."

"I thought you were supposed to be on my side, Edith."

"It's not a question of sides. It's a question of realities—of what is going to happen unless you come to your senses quickly." Edith jerked her head back as if she had detected an unpleasant odor around him. "Think it over."

She turned on an expensive heel and marched off. Tree hobbled away in the opposite direction.

He didn't get very far.

"Mr. Callister, there you are." The honeyed voice of T. Emmett Hawkins.

"Mr. Hawkins," Tree said.

"I've been trying to get hold of you, sir." He guided Tree into a corner. Today, he wore an orange bow tie. It was not every man who could pull off an orange bow tie, Tree thought.

"Why are you walking so funny?"

"I hurt my ribs," Tree said.

"In the pursuit of proving Mrs. Traven's innocence, I hope."

"In pursuit, yes," Tree said. "However, I have yet to catch up to her innocence."

"I'm sorry to hear that, Mr. Callister."

"In fact, I would say she's looking a little guiltier than she did before."

Hawkins looked disappointed. "Why is that, Mr. Callister?"

"An ex-convict named Tony Dodge."

Hawkins looked at him blankly. "I have no idea who that is."

"Well, I think we had better find out more about him."

Hawkins moved back a few paces as though he too had caught a bad smell around Tree. "How much have you told the police?"

"I haven't told the police anything, but as you can imagine, Mr. Hawkins, I'm under quite a bit of pressure to tell them something. In fact my lawyer tells me I'm on my way to jail if I don't."

"To be frank, Mr. Callister, it will be very difficult to ask my client anything along those lines."

"Why is that?"

"Because any conversations that take place inside the Lee County jail are liable to be recorded."

"Even with attorneys?"

"I don't want to take the chance. Please don't worry about this Dodge character. Just continue on. She's counting on you, Mr. Callister. You're all she's got."

"I'm all she's got? That's not much of anything," Tree said.

"No, it certainly isn't." It was Hawkins turn to march off. Everyone was walking away from him this morning after delivering a well-honed insult or threat.

There was no justice.

26

I watched *Rio Bravo* last night," Rex Baxter said after Tree raised his shirt so Rex could inspect his bruised ribs.

"I still don't know what to make of it. Is it one of the greatest westerns ever made? Howard Hawks' signature work? Or is it this goofily entertaining hodgepodge that, among other unlikely things, asks us to buy Ricky Nelson as a tough-as-nails gunslinger?"

"What do you think?" Tree said.

Rex poked at Tree's rib cage. Tree let out a yelp. "To be honest, *Rio Bravo* is a little bit of both. I mean, you can't help but be entertained by it. Certainly the byplay between the Duke and Angie Dickinson as the saloon girl, Feathers, is wondrous, right up there with Bogart and Bacall in Hawks' *To Have and Have Not*."

"I'm not talking about *Rio Bravo*," Tree said. "I'm talking about my ribs. Do they look broken or not?"

Rex peered more closely, as if he had X-ray vision. "The thing I wonder about *Rio Bravo*, you know, the Duke and Walter Brennan and Dean Martin as the drunk, they've got Claude Atkins in jail and they're holding him, waiting for the arrival of the U.S. marshal who's presumably going to take Claude Atkins away, right?"

"Quit poking at my ribs," Tree said. "It hurts."

Rex straightened. "John Russell plays the evil rancher-father who wants to spring his son from the Duke's jail. What I can't quite figure, why doesn't John Russell just wait until the marshal leaves town with Claude Akins, and then jump him? It would be a whole lot easier than going up against the Duke in a fortified sheriff's office."

"Do you think my ribs are broken or not, Rex?" Tree sounded exasperated.

"How would I know, Tree? There's bruising there. It doesn't look good, I can tell you that much. What does Freddie say?"

"She thinks I should go to the doctor."

"That's sound advice. Why don't you do that?"

"Because if I listen to sound advice right now, I'm in trouble."

"You're already in trouble," Rex said.

"Also, a doctor might ask too many questions."

"Just don't come across any more dead bodies," Rex said. "It's not good for tourism."

"I'll keep that in mind," Tree said.

"I hate to be critical, Tree. We've known each other a long time, after all. But in general you have not been good for tourism on the island."

"Boy, I can always count on you for support, Rex."

"In *Rio Bravo* John Wayne doesn't want anyone's help. He's got a problem, he fixes it himself. He can't stand the fact that Dean Martin's a drunk. He thinks Dino should quit whining and stand on his own two feet."

"Maybe you're watching too many John Wayne movies," Tree said.

"Stand on your own two feet," Rex said. "That's what John Wayne would do."

"John Wayne doesn't have broken ribs," Tree said.

"Possible broken ribs," Rex amended.

After Rex finally departed in mid grumble for a meeting to discuss final preparations for the upcoming Kiwanis spaghetti dinner, Tree turned to his computer and Googled Aksel Baldur. According to Wikipedia, Axel was born in Turku, Finland, a town on the southwest coast at the mouth of the Aura River.

His parents emigrated to the U.S. when he was two years old. He grew up on a farm in rural Minnesota, dreaming of better things. Graduating from the University of Minnesota at Duluth with a business degree, he somehow scraped together enough money to buy a floundering Duluth clothing company.

Over the next ten years, Baldur moved his company to Chicago where it specialized in inexpensive women's clothes. Its success made him a multi-millionaire. The money fueled an outrageous lifestyle that provided the notoriety his fashion sense never could. The abundance of available women and drugs inevitably brought trouble.

Six former employees had launched sexual harassment suits against him. Two models accused him in civil suits of fathering their children. Most serious of all were the allegations that he had sex with underage prostitutes.

Three fifteen-year-old Jamaican girls claimed Aksel had lured them to his Negril Beach house, plied them with alcohol and drugs, and then raped them. Baldur denied the charges, and then quickly settled out of court with the girls' families. The criminal cases against him went away.

His appetites, he said, grew out of his terrible childhood. Victimized by a monster father, he told the *Los Angeles Times* that he and his sister were always hungry as children, sometimes existing on little more than the boiled potatoes.

Aksel claimed in an *Esquire* magazine interview that he was eight years old when he watched his father kill his mother. He told *Esquire* his father had strangled her and then ordered Aksel into the basement to watch her die. His mother was buried in the garden behind the house. His father forced him to help with the burial.

Aksel's father died in 1989. The mother, according to the magazine, was never reported missing. "My life has not been easy," Aksel said. "I work hard and I play hard in order to keep the monsters away."

Tree wondered if, in trying so hard to push the monsters away, Aksel Baldur had become one of the monsters. You would hide from the monster if he came after you, would you not? Maybe that's what Chris and Kendra were doing.

Hiding.

But where?

27

The house Ray Dayton owned in Naples backed onto the beach off Gulf Shore Boulevard. It was a rambling one story structure with a red tile roof, surrounded by a wall. Tree parked on the street in front of the house.

He eased himself gingerly out of the Beetle so as not to ignite the sleeping pain inside his rib cage. Despite his best efforts, the pain reawakened as he hobbled across the drive to the lacquered entrance door and rang the bell.

From inside, a cacophony of chimes rose to announce the visitor. No one heeded the call. Tree went around the side of the house and through a gate that opened onto a wide terrace intersected by a pool the size of a lake. Beyond the pool, the Gulf of Mexico came into sharp focus. From this vantage point, Tree could see a lone figure on the beach propped in an Adirondack chair.

He circled around the pool until he found a short flight of stone stairs leading down to the beach.

Chris, wearing sunglasses and bright paisley bathing trunks, sat in the chair with his back to Tree. Two empty beer cans lay in the sand beside his chair. Chris was working on the third as Tree positioned himself in front of his son.

It took Chris a moment to register his father's presence. He removed the glasses and then used his hand to shade his eyes so he could get a better look.

"How come you're standing so funny?" he said in a lazy slur.

"I broke some ribs."

"You should go to a hospital."

"I wanted to find you first."

"Is that so?" Chris did not appear surprised that his father might be looking for him. "How did you find me?"

Tree did not want to say that he encountered Chris's wife with the Ray Man, that he knew about the Naples house and took a wild guess. Instead, he said, "That's why I'm a detective."

Chris gave him a crooked grin. "But Dad, you're not a very good detective."

Tree let the insult wash off him. "Good enough to find you," he said.

"I guess you are at that," Chris agreed. "After all, here you are."

"Where's Kendra?" Tree said.

For a moment, Tree wasn't sure Chris had heard him. Then his son waved his hand and said, "Gone, finito. Finished."

"What? You and Kendra split up?"

"Kendra did the splitting, man. But that's Kendra, isn't it? Last in. First out. That's my baby."

"I'm sorry, Chris."

Chris put his sunglasses back on. "I don't think you and Freddie ever liked her."

"That's not true."

"Everyone else liked her. Everyone wanted to sleep with her. Men and women. Didn't make any difference—not to them, maybe not to Kendra either."

He took a long swig of his beer.

Tree said, "Is she with Aksel Baldur?"

Chris looked at him sharply. "How do you know about him?"

"Is that where she's gone?"

"She's afraid of Aksel. I don't think she went back to him."

"Why is she afraid of Aksel, Chris? Why are the two of you afraid of him?"

"Because he is evil, and we were stupid and gullible, and we should never have got ourselves involved with him or rather, Kendra shouldn't have."

"But Kendra did."

"She thought she could twist him around her little finger like she did every other guy she ever met. To a certain extent she could—but then she couldn't and that's when the trouble started."

"The two of you were in business with him."

Chris finished his beer. "I need another beer," he said. "And I need to get out of this sun." He squinted up at Tree. "You gonna stick around, Dad?"

"Sure."

"Detective Dad, huh? Well, don't think for a minute you can help me. I'm good and screwed. Better stay away from me."

"Let's go up to the house," Tree said. "We'll get you another beer."

"Sure, Dad. Let's have a beer. Father and son. Oh, wait. You can't have a beer. You don't drink. Perfect dad."

Tree thought of the days when he did drink. Not so perfect then.

Chris dropped the empty beer can to the sand, pushed himself to his feet and began to take uncertain steps toward the house. Tree bent down, picked up the beer cans, and then followed him across the beach, up the steps to the terrace. The sliding doors facing the pool were open. By the time Tree entered the kitchen, Chris already had the refrigerator open and was drawing out another beer.

In the dimness, Chris appeared like a dark brown question mark. Tree had never seen him so tanned. Skin cancer, he thought. But maybe that was the least of Chris's problems.

"What are you going to do?" Tree asked.

Chris brushed past, snapping the cap open. He swayed a bit as he disappeared from the kitchen.

"Chris?" Tree called. No answer.

Tree found him by the window in a low-ceilinged sitting room, holding the beer, staring out at the ocean.

"Chris? Did you hear me?"

Turning, Chris appeared to see his father for the first time. "What's that, Dad?"

"I asked you what you're going to do."

He shrugged. "I don't know."

"How long can you stay here?"

Another shrug. "As long as I want to, I suppose. Ray doesn't seem to mind."

"Ray Dayton doesn't mind?"

"He's a friend." As though the Ray Man was a friend to all.

Tree leaned forward and plucked the beer can from Chris's fingers. That produced an unexpected flare of anger. "What the hell do you think you're doing?"

"Tell me about Aksel Baldur, about being in business with him."

"What do you want to know?"

"Why a wealthy clothing designer would be interested in a small Chicago online dating service."

Chris gave him a smirk, as though Tree should know better. "Kendra."

"Or maybe it wasn't a real dating service."

Chris blinked a couple of times. "What would it be, then?"

"A front? For supplying young women to Baldur and other wealthy clients?"

Chris didn't say anything.

Tree said, "Who's Sasha?"

Chris's face dropped in surprise. He said quietly, "Dad, don't get mixed up in this."

"I'm already mixed up in it," Tree said. "Who is Sasha?"

"Sasha Itsov. Aksel's man."

"What about a guy named Tony Dodge?"

Chris looked blank. "I don't know him."

"How about Elizabeth Traven, do you know who she is?"

"Yes, of course. She started all this. She's the one who knew a couple named Reno O'Hara and Dara Rait," he said.

Tree knew them, too—bad actors involved in the body parts business. Before that, Dara and Reno had been in the sex trade.

"Reno and Dara are dead," Tree said.

"Yes, but the network they established remained pretty much in place. Elizabeth restarted it. Baldur was looking for women, so were some of his friends. He introduced Kendra to the mix. He had met her when she was working for *Playboy*. She became his local conduit. Elizabeth brought the women up from Mexico. Kendra made sure they were taken care of in Chicago. Red Rose. That's what they called the business. High-class sex. Very lucrative."

Tree took out his wallet and extracted the card he had found near Traven's body. "Is this your business card?"

Chris peered at it. "The card Elizabeth and Kendra use, yeah."

Elizabeth should have known better, he thought. But she had said she would do whatever was necessary. Trafficking women was necessary, apparently.

"What about Elizabeth's husband?" Tree said.

"Brand? I hear he was furious when he got out of jail and found out what Elizabeth was up to. That's the reason she killed him, I suppose."

"How deep are you in it?"

He shrugged. "Deep enough. By the time I realized what Kendra was up to, it was too late. Or I convinced myself it was too late. I don't know. Kendra is hard to resist once she decides on something."

"Except everything seems to be coming apart."

Chris lowered his head and muttered, "Baldur's crazy. A psycho. He gets these ideas in his head and he won't listen to anyone."

"What about Ray Dayton?"

"What about him?"

"How does he figure in this?"

Chris shook his head. "Like I said, he's a friend."

Some friend, Tree thought.

28

"Tree, you can hardly move," Freddie said as she helped him across the terrace and into a chair near the pool.

"I'm fine," he said.

"No you are not. You've got to get to a doctor."

"I haven't had time," Tree said, arranging himself so that he was more comfortable.

He told Freddie about his afternoon encounter with Chris. He did not tell her Chris was staying at Ray's place in Naples. He left out the parts about Red Rose and Chris and Kendra's involvement in the high-end sex trade. What Freddie did not know could not put her into a compromising position if the police came around.

By the time he finished, Freddie had armed herself with a glass of chardonnay. Now she leveled a hard stare at him. "There's a whole lot here you're not telling me. I don't like it when bad things are happening to you, but I like it even less when you don't tell me."

"Listen, I've got an idea, why don't we talk about what's happening in your life for a change. You haven't told me how things are going at work for a long time. That used to be the main topic of conversation around here."

"Before you started getting into trouble." The hint of a smile.

"Come on, Freddie. Tell me about your day."

A frown replaced the smile. "Well, let me see. I'm worried about the business, and I'm concerned about Ray."

"What's Ray doing?"

"It's what he's not doing. He's not there a lot of the time. When he is, he's distracted. His marriage is in trouble."

"I heard something about that."

"You did?"

"Are they splitting?"

"I think he's on the verge of doing something crazy like that, yes."

"It seems to me Ray's always on the verge of something crazy. Remember how he carried the torch for you—maybe he still does."

"No, I'm old news. There's a new love in his life, I believe."

Tree said carefully, "Any idea who it is?"

"No, but there's someone."

Freddie was right, of course. There was someone. It did not take much to guess that Ray's new love was his own daughter-in-law.

———

Lying in bed later that night, Tree heard something in the other room. Someone was moving around out there.

He slipped out of bed and, bones aching, limped out to the living room. A figure came into view, a tall, heavyset cowboy, imposing in the gloom. He wore faded jeans, scuffed and dusty cowboy boots, and a dark blue cavalry blouse with yellow buttons. His craggy face appeared drawn and tired. He held a wide-brimmed Stetson.

The cowboy nodded when he saw Tree and gave a crooked smile. "There you are," he said in a lazy drawl. "Wondered if you were gonna show up."

"What are you doing here?"

"Just passing through. Heard you were in trouble, thought I'd see if I could help out."

The cowboy lowered himself into an armchair, stretching out his left leg. He placed his hat on the floor beside him.

"I'm not sure what you can do," Tree said.

"Well, I happen to know a thing or two when it comes to getting out of a tight spot," the cowboy said.

"I suppose you do at that," Tree agreed. "But I'm not sure how that applies to me. I'm nothing like you."

"No, you're not, and I suppose the kind of rugged individualism I represent is out of fashion. But listen, Tree, I've had plenty of family problems, too. No matter how tough you are, no matter how much you refuse to back down from things, family can still mess you up."

"Boy, you've got that right," Tree said. "My son is in terrible trouble, and I blame myself for that. I was a lousy father. I should have been home taking care of him and my other kids, but I was working or leaning against a bar somewhere. If I'd been around more, things might have been different, and he wouldn't have gone so wrong."

"Or maybe it wouldn't have made any difference," the cowboy said. "Who can say? You do your best, and the chips fall where they fall, and there's not a lot you can do about it."

"That's it?" Tree said. He felt his anger rising. "'The chips fall?' That's the best you can do?"

"Listen, sooner or later, the kids have to make their own way in life, like the rest of us. What? You had a great father?"

"No, he wasn't so great," Tree admitted. "Still isn't so great. But that's no excuse. I should have done better."

"Maybe you should have, but you didn't. So what are you going to do now?"

"You're the hero," Tree said angrily. "You tell me."

"Heroes save the day, shoot the bad guys, overcome the odds. You notice they don't have much to do with families."

"No," Tree said.

"That's because where families are concerned, there ain't no heroes, son. No heroes at all."

Tree jerked awake. Freddie stirred beside him. She laid her hand gently on his arm. "Are you all right?"

"I was talking to him just now," Tree said.

"Who were you talking to?"

"I'm not sure, but I think it was John Wayne."

"John Wayne's dead, Tree," Freddie said in the calming voice she employed at times like this. "Go back to sleep."

29

HOT pasta!" cried Rex Baxter, sweating profusely as he lugged a steaming metal pot into the Sanibel Community Center kitchen.

Kiwanis Club members wearing white aprons, moved quickly out of the way as Rex passed. Rex was notorious for spilling pasta at past Kiwanis spaghetti dinners.

Rex grunted and sweated his way into the main hall where early arrivals crowded rows of trestle tables. The wait line already snaked out the door and across the parking lot. Kiwanians served eager customers plastic plates piled with spaghetti and meatballs prepared by cooks toiling beneath a marquee in the parking lot. Tree was one of four Salad Guys fixing shards of lettuce dusted with croutons, soaked in a balsamic dressing and presented in white plastic tubs.

Tree was tasked with garnishing the croutons on the individual salads, the final, crucial part of the salad process, Tree noted, and not to be taken lightly.

"Everyone doing all right in here?" Rex, having delivered his pasta, reappeared in the kitchen, teeth clenched, as if he was leading a police raid on the place. Everyone said they were doing fine. Rex disappeared outside.

"I thought Ray was in charge again this year," Tree said to Todd Jackson.

Todd said, "Ray hasn't shown."

"Ray missing the chance to run something? He must have been hit by a truck," said Mitch Traynor, another of the salad guys, a lawyer when he wasn't emptying lettuce into plastic bowls set out on metal trays.

"I doubt Ray was hit by a truck," Todd said. "Maybe hit by something else, but not a truck."

An hour later, word came back to the kitchen that the wait line now stretched out through the parking lot as far as the roadway. The Salad Guys picked up the pace. Rex sweated more, and yelled "HOT pasta!" even louder than before. The heat was definitely on.

"We're running out of salad!" Todd announced as he set more plastic bowls on a tray.

"What?" Rex was back in the kitchen, eyes bulging.

"Looks like we're almost out of salad, Rex," Todd said.

"Damn!" roared Rex. "Who ordered the salad? Ray was supposed to look after that. Where the hell is he, anyway?"

"Missing in action," Mitch the lawyer said.

Todd chuckled knowingly. Tree looked at him. Knowingly about what?

Rex continued to glare. "He said he'd be here. Ray told me he had everything taken care of. Not to worry."

Tree opened the big stainless steel refrigerator behind him. It was stuffed with salad bags.

"More salad here," he called out. Everyone looked relieved. Rex's eyes stopped bulging so much.

"Good work, Salad Guys!" he shouted. Todd made a face at Rex's back disappearing out the door.

Two hours later, the hall was still filled with eager spaghetti eaters, but the lineup had disappeared. The Salad Guys were ordered to cut back. Tree leaned against the counter sipping a Diet Coke, talking to Todd Jackson.

"Best year yet," Todd said. "It's because you're here, Tree. People like the way you sprinkle those croutons."

"I think it's because Ray isn't here," Mitch said coming over, beer in hand. "It runs much more smoothly with Rex yelling and screaming, than it does with Ray screaming and yelling."

"I bet I know why Ray isn't here," Todd said.

Everyone looked at him.

"Well, you know don't you?" Todd said.

"I don't know," Tree said.

"The rumors."

"What rumors?"

"That Ray's off the reservation," Todd said.

Tree looked at him. "What's that mean?"

"What do you think it means? It means Ray is being a bad boy."

"You mean he's fooling around?" Mitch said.

"Some hottie half his age, I hear."

"You sure about this?" Tree said.

"One of the guys who works with me, Ace Crosby. He was cleaning carpets at 1822 Woodring Rd. yesterday. Ace was packing the equipment into the truck when who comes out of the house across the street but the Ray Man and his babe. A real hottie, according to Ace. I heard Ray grumbling a while back about a house on Woodring he had to kick his tenants out of. Maybe that's the place."

Tree looked out the window over the sink. It was nearly dark. He now he had a pretty good idea where Kendra was.

And who she was with.

The anger rose again, red hot this time. Not like him. But then nothing was like him these days.

"You okay, Tree?" Todd Jackson said.

Tree started to take off his apron.

30

When you thought you could not go further once you turned onto Dixie Beach Road from Periwinkle Way, there was Woodring Road snaking to the left along a thin strip of land poking between San Carlos Bay and Lady-finger Lake. The road was unpaved and unlit, and for a time Tree didn't think there were houses along this stretch. Then he passed a wood-frame bungalow. Beyond it was a ramshackle, two-story structure with weather-beaten wood siding. The house stood across the street from eighteen twenty-two.

Tree parked in the drive beside a Dodge Durango and got out. He went along a gravel walkway to the entrance. The door was ajar. Tree pushed it further open and eased inside. A narrow passageway led into a sitting room.

Chris slumped in an easy chair at the far end of the room. For a terrible moment, Tree thought his son was dead. But as he approached, Chris's head moved so that the light shifted off his glasses. He opened bleary eyes and gazed up at Tree.

"Oh, God," he said. "Oh, God."

Tree bent over him. "Where's Kendra?"

Chris's face crumpled, and he began to sob.

"Chris. Tell me where Kendra is."

"Upstairs," Chris said.

"Stay here."

"Don't go up there, Dad." Chris sobbed harder.

Stairs led up to the second floor. Double doors opened onto the master bedroom.

Clothing in pale springtime colors trailed across a plank floor adjacent to an unmade king-size bed. A woman wearing a black thong lay on a bright blue Duvet, her face buried in a pillow. Tree's eyes went to the rose tattoo at the base of her spine.

The red, red rose of Kendra Callister.

Tree called her name. She did not answer. She was never going to answer anyone again. He saw what looked like a belt around her neck. Someone had used the belt to strangle her.

Tree backed away trying not to think the worst, trying not to think that his son, sobbing away downstairs, had killed his wife.

Trying not to think what everyone else was going to be thinking.

Chris was still in the chair in the living room, his face streaked with tears. His whole body shook. Tree wrapped his arms around him and said, "Listen to me, Chris, just try to calm down, okay? Take deep breaths."

For the first time since Tree could remember, Chris actually listened to him and gulped for air.

"How long ago did you get here, Chris?"

"Maybe ten minutes," he said.

"Was anyone else here?"

Chris shook his head.

"I need to ask you this, okay? I need to ask you if you did this. Chris? Did you kill Kendra?"

He sobbed some more and shook his head. "I walked in, found her upstairs, on the bed—"

"Why did you come here?"

"She called. She said she wanted to see me."

"About what?"

"She didn't say. She told me where she was and asked me to come over. I had a hell of a time finding this place. It took me forever."

"Did anyone see you come in?"

Chris had calmed. He brushed at the streaming tears as he shook his head. "I don't think so."

"Is that your vehicle outside? Or is it Kendra's?"

"It's mine."

"Where did Kendra park?"

"I don't know. Her car is back at the house in Naples, I guess."

"All right, what I want you to do is get out of here, go back to my place."

"I shouldn't leave her," Chris said.

"If you don't go, and they find you here, they are probably going to arrest you. You're the husband. Your wife is dead, and here you are."

"It doesn't look good," Chris admitted.

"Get in your car. Drive over to the house. I'll call Freddie and tell her you're coming."

"What are you going to do?"

"I'm going to take care of this."

31

As soon as Chris left, Tree went back up to the bedroom.

He eased around the bed, not wanting to look at Kendra. He felt empty, drained of any emotion. He had a job to do, and he would do it. The mourning and guilt could wait for later.

He found Kendra's brown leather shoulder bag on the floor in the corner and used a tissue to unzip it. He rummaged through its contents, poking away with the pen he carried.

The purse contained a set of car keys, a wallet, a vial of NYC Hamptons perfume, a Blackberry. Tree used the tissue to ease the wallet out. It was long and elegant in glossy brown leather. It contained one hundred dollars in cash, as well as credit cards, a driver's license—and a laminated Red Rose business card.

He slipped the card into his pocket before replacing the wallet. He then fished out her Blackberry phone still using the tissue. The Blackberry was password-protected and so he couldn't get into it.

He went into the bathroom. The counter was filled with her toiletries: eyeliner, mascara, eye shadow, foundations, face powders, perfumes.

A plastic makeup bag with a paisley design was propped against the mirror. Tree opened it and used his pen to move around a makeup brush, blush-on, a mirror, and a Data Stick Pro USB flash drive.

He dropped the flash drive into his pocket and then found a face cloth in the bathroom closet and used it to clean any surfaces his son might have touched. It struck him that in addition to wiping away traces of Chris, he was probably doing the same thing for Kendra's killer. Unless, of course, Chris was the killer. No, that couldn't be. He must believe in his son's innocence. And because he believed, he could rationalize what he was doing. He could convince himself he was doing what was necessary to protect his boy.

When he finished, Tree went back downstairs and rummaged in the kitchen until he found a box of business envelopes and stamps. He addressed one of them to himself, folded an advertising flyer for Jerry's Foods three times, dropped the flash drive and the Red Rose business card into its fold, shoved the flyer into the envelope and sealed it. He fixed a stamp to the outside of the envelope and then left the house and crossed to eighteen twenty-two and placed the envelope in the mailbox.

He reentered the house and called 911 on his cell. He told the operator that someone was dead in a frame house on Woodring Road. He hung up without answering any more questions.

Then he called Freddie. "Kendra is dead," he said.

"What? How?"

"I don't have a lot of time to talk now," Tree said. "The police are going to be here any moment. Chris will be at our house shortly. He's pretty shaken up. After the police talk to me, they're going to talk to you and Chris. I'm going to need you to verify his story."

"Which is?"

"That he's been with us since this afternoon. Simple. Nothing complicated."

"But that isn't true," Freddie said in that frighteningly realistic tone she adopted when the subject of lying came up.

"I know it isn't," Tree said.

"You want me to lie to the police."

"Otherwise, in all likelihood, Chris will be arrested for his wife's murder."

Freddie paused for a long time before she said, "You should not do this."

"Freddie, please." Tree did not try to hide his desperation. "This one time, don't argue. I need you to do this."

"I'm just afraid you are digging a hole that we can't get out of."

"Freddie."

"Here's Chris now. Call me later."

When he started to object, Freddie hung up.

Without agreeing to anything.

32

At four o'clock in the morning, Detective Own Markfield said, "So here we go again, Tree. I arrive at a
murder scene and presto! You appear."

Tree was too tired to respond. This must be what it's
like to be worn down to the point where you are willing to
admit to anything: yes, yes. I am Sanibel Island's first serial
killer. Sixty years old and exhausted, but ready to kill again.
Now, please, let me get some sleep.

He looked blearily around the police conference room.
By now it was all too familiar: the stale air, the sense of
claustrophobia, the dryness in his throat, the numb, hope-
less feeling that comes from being in big trouble.

They had been at this for hours. He had told various
police interrogators a more-or-less factual version of the
events that had led him to the house on Woodring Road
and Kendra's body. However, he had left out the part where
he found his son in the house.

"Here's the thing, Tree." Markfield had removed his
suit jacket, loosened his tie, and rolled up his shirt sleeves,
ready to do the heavy lifting.

"You're at this spaghetti dinner. You hear some things that lead you to this house on Woodring Road belonging to Ray Dayton, your wife's boss."

"That's correct," Tree said. "Just like I've told you three or four times."

"You know that your son and daughter-in-law are in a great deal of financial difficulty. Now here she is shacked up in the house belonging to a man you dislike intensely, a man who apparently you've come to blows with in the past. Gets you pretty steamed up. Does all that sound accurate so far?"

"Maybe I wasn't all that steamed up," Tree said. "More along the lines of, I couldn't believe what the two of them were up to."

"You get to the house, and now you're boiling. This is your son's wife, and she's fooling around with *your wife's boss*. So you go charging in, and there's Kendra, not wearing much of anything, waiting for lover boy. I wouldn't blame you for seeing red. Losing it. The two of you argue, fight. You grab her and the next thing you know, she's on the bed, face down, and you've got that belt around her neck, and she's not moving."

Markfield paused. Silence crowded the room.

Tree said, "Let's see, first it was me murdering Brand Traven. Now I'm killing my daughter-in-law. I'm having trouble keeping track of all the carnage."

The door opened and a sleepy-eyed Edith Goldman poked her head in.

Markfield frowned and said, "We're not finished, Edith."

"Yes, you are."

Edith stepped further into the room. She wore jeans and a blue blazer over a white blouse. "Tree, I want you to stand up and leave." She glared at Markfield. "If you're going to charge my client, do it now. Otherwise, you have no reason to hold him, and he's out of here."

That brought Markfield to his feet. "All right, Tree, you can go. But at the moment you are our number one suspect. Be aware of that."

"If you want to speak to my client again, you call me first," Edith said.

Markfield kept his eyes on Tree. "Don't leave the island. Understand?"

Tree looked at Edith. "My client will go where he damned well pleases," she said.

33

No reporters waited for Tree and Edith as they came out of police headquarters. One of the few good things about a murder on Sanibel Island at this time of the morning—the local media were sleeping soundly, unaware that a former *Playboy* model had been found dead in a house belonging to one of the island's most prominent residents.

Edith said, "God, Tree, can you possibly get yourself into any more trouble?"

"I don't think so, Edith. But then I never expected to get in this much, so I guess you never know with me."

Edith shook her head. "Let me see. They've already got you on aiding and abetting in connection with one murder. Now you are the prime suspect in a second murder. I would say that's about as bad as it gets."

"Thanks, Edith," Tree said. "I really appreciate your support."

"I'm just trying to be honest with you," she said. "Incidentally, they impounded your car."

Tree groaned. "They keep doing that. I don't think they want me, they want my Beetle."

"On top of being deprived of a night's sleep, I suppose I have to drive you home."

"You are a heck of a lawyer, Edith."

"I'll remind you of that when you're sitting in jail for the next twenty-five years."

Freddie was dressed and waiting for him when they arrived at Andy Rosse Lane. Edith drove off. Tree wrapped his arms around his wife.

"The police were here talking to Chris," she said. "They left about twenty minutes ago."

"Where is he now?"

"In bed. Sound asleep. He was pretty exhausted."

"How is he doing?"

"Not good. I'm not sure how well he did with the police, either."

"It can't have gone too badly since I'm the one on the verge of being charged with Kendra's murder."

"You're not serious," Freddie said.

"Even if I'm not, the police are."

"But why would you murder your own daughter-in-law?"

"If you believe the police, I found out she was having an affair with Ray Dayton. I went around to the house on Woodring Road where she was staying, confronted her, and choked her to death."

Freddie had gone pale. "Don't tell me Ray and Kendra were having an affair."

"I don't know about an affair, but they were having sex."

Freddie was shaking her head. "Chris thinks Ray is a friend."

"Some friend."

Freddie shook her head some more. "I don't believe it."

"Sure you do, Freddie. You suspected something wasn't right with Ray."

"But not my own daughter-in-law!" Her voice rose in unaccustomed anger. "What the hell was he thinking?"

"He wasn't thinking. That's the whole point with the Kendras of the world. They act as some sort of heat shield that stops guys like Ray Dayton thinking."

"What made you go over there tonight?"

"This was a joke at the Kiwanis dinner," Tree said. "I was furious. I suppose I wanted to catch her with Ray. I suppose I had some crazy idea about trying to protect Chris."

"All the more reason, why someone might think you killed her."

"Yes."

Her eyes searched his. "But you didn't kill her, Tree. Not my husband. Not you."

"No, it wasn't me," Tree said.

"So why am I so suspicious you're still not telling me everything?"

"You're right, I'm not."

"I thought you were going to stop doing that."

"Was I? It's so late, I can't remember."

"Tree. That's enough."

Tree took a deep breath before he said: "Chris was in the house when I got there."

That turned Freddie paler. "Don't tell me he killed Kendra."

"He says he didn't. I believe him."

"So you made it look as though you might have done it."

"Something like that."

"Oh, God, Tree," she said in a choked voice.

There were tears in her eyes. Freddie, crying. He couldn't remember the last time that happened. He took her in his arms. She laid her head against his shoulder. Her tears dampened his shirt. "It's going to be all right," he said.

"No," she said with a vehemence that surprised him. "No, it's not."

34

Rex said, "In *Hondo*, John Wayne plays this weird guy named Hondo Lane who has a mangy dog and who used to live with the Apaches.

"Hondo falls in love with a rancher's wife played by Geraldine Page. She's crazy about him, but can't do anything about it because she's already married and has a son. Hondo solves that problem by killing her husband. Since Geraldine is in love with Hondo, she brushes off the guy's death in about two seconds. Then the Apaches show up; there's a shoot-out, and then Hondo and the married woman he made a widow set off together for California. The dog and the kid come along, too."

"You gotta wonder what's going to happen to a couple like that," Todd Jackson said.

"What do you mean?" Rex said.

"For example, Hondo's idea of being a dad is to toss the woman's son into a deep river and the kid literally has to sink or swim. What happens when the kid becomes a teenager and comes home late? What does Hondo do then? Shoot him? Then there's the whole thing about the murdered husband. She's gotta wake up every morning and think, 'Here's the son of a bitch who killed my husband. Maybe I'm next.' Not a recipe for happiness, if you ask me."

"A lot of those 1950s movies would set up these great dilemmas—what do you do when the man you love kills your husband?—and then ignore them," Rex said. "But then that's the thing about those movies, isn't it? You shoot some Apaches and live happily ever after."

Todd said, "I hate pictures where you realize that everyone you're watching on the screen is dead."

"That cuts you out of a lot of movies," Rex said. He looked over at Tree who was standing at the office window. "Hey, Tree, your coffee's getting cold."

"That TV truck is still out there," Tree said.

"They're waiting for you to kill someone," Rex said. "You're the Hondo of Sanibel Island."

"I know this isn't funny, I know I shouldn't laugh," said Todd Jackson, laughing.

Tree came back to his desk and sat down heavily. He reached for his coffee.

"What can you do?" Rex said. "I'm best friends with the guy who is single-handedly destroying tourism on this island."

"Sorry about that," Tree said.

"It's worse than burnt pancakes on a Sunday morning, as we used to say in Oklahoma."

The telephone rang.

"Aren't you going to answer it?" Rex asked.

"It's a reporter," Tree said.

"You're more famous than Mel Gibson," Rex said.

"Or Lindsay Lohan," Todd said.

"But Lindsay is cuter," Rex said.

Rex and Todd finished their coffee and left a few minutes later. Tree sat at his desk. The tension drained away for the first time since he had arrived at the office, trailed by reporters and photographers who now were awake and anxious for comment on Kendra's murder. He told them he had nothing to say. Several reporters argued that he was a former newspaperman and therefore should have plenty to say.

But say what? Tree wondered. How did he feel? Wasn't that the question everyone always asked? He had asked it a couple of thousand times himself during his years as a reporter. A stupid question.

He felt lousy. How else could he feel?

The phone rang some more. He ignored it in favor of staring out the window while he tried to extract something profound from recent events. His mind was blank. There was nothing profound about what he had done—artfully trapping himself so that if he told the truth, his son might well go to jail for the rest of his life. If he continued to lie, he was headed for jail. Real life had a way of canceling out profundity.

He turned to the mail piled on his desk, sifting through the bills and advertising flyers until he found the envelope that he had mailed from Woodring Road. He tore it open and the USB flash from Kendra's makeup bag along with the Red Rose business card dropped to the desk.

He picked up the stick and inserted it into the side of his PC. The computer asked him if he wanted to download the twenty photos it said were on the flash. Tree agreed, and the computer went to work.

When the downloading was complete, Tree clicked on the file and opened the photographs as a slide show. There were photos of Kendra and other beautiful young women, mugging for the camera, showing lots of leg and cleavage, against a party backdrop.

Then a sweaty, red-faced Aksel Baldur appeared, posed with his arm around Kendra and Elizabeth Traven. Elizabeth stared fixedly at the camera. Kendra snuggled close to Axel, flashing one of her thousand watt smiles. Next, Baldur was kissing Kendra. Elizabeth was nowhere to be seen. That was followed by Kendra nude, lying on her stomach. Aksel, also nude, was on top of her, teeth gritted as he twisted a belt around her neck.

The ringing telephone startled him. Tree looked at the digital display: The Lee County Jail. Tree picked up the receiver and a voice said, "Mr. Callister, this is Elizabeth Traven calling."

Tree sat back in his chair, not taking his eyes off the photo on the screen. "Yes, Mrs. Traven."

"How are you? Obviously, I've heard about your daughter-in-law's death."

Yes," Tree said.

"You are aware, of course, that these telephone conversations are recorded."

"Yes, I am."

"But you are all right?"

"Yes," Tree said.

"And you are continuing with your investigation?"

"I'm on top of it."

Elizabeth paused before she said, "It's just that my attorney has voiced disappointment about the level of cooperation he has so far received from you."

Tree continued to study Kendra and Aksel—and the belt twisted around her neck.

"I'm on it."

"Do me a favor, will you? Call Emmett Hawkins and bring him up to date."

"Did you know her?"

"Know who?"

"My daughter-in-law, Kendra."

Elizabeth hesitated a couple of beats too long before she said, "How would I know her?"

"I thought perhaps you had met, maybe at a party in Sarasota."

More silence before she replied, "No."

The line went dead. Tree restarted the Kendra slide-show. Kendra once again flared on the computer screen, beautiful, apparently delighted to have Aksel Baldur choking her.

35

"Is that the guy?" Ferne Clowers said.

Not far away, Sasha parked a Lincoln Towncar, got out and walked across the deserted mall to the double glass doors leading to his office.

"That's him," Tree said as Sasha went inside.

He was seated in the rear of a green van with Ferne in the passenger seat while Slippery Street was all but lost behind the steering wheel. He did not look happy.

Ferne had picked Tree up at his office twenty minutes after he called her. Slippery was a surprise. "Depending on what happens, we may need a good driver," said Ferne.

Slippery had just scowled. Ferne told him to get moving. Slippery had mumbled something dark Tree couldn't make out before starting the engine. He mumbled something darker when Tree told Slippery to drive to Sarasota.

Three hours later, parked in the mall, waiting on Sasha, Slippery remained the picture of misery. "How long we gonna sit here?"

"As long as it takes, Slippery," answered Ferne patiently.

Slippery squirmed in his seat. "I don't like sitting around. I'm the sort of guy who's gotta move, get something happening."

"What do you suggest we do?" Tree asked.

"I say we go in there and open up a can of whoop-ass on that dude, get what we want out of him, and move on."

"I would like to do this in a way that doesn't land us in prison," Tree said.

"Hey, prison's not so bad," Slippery said. "Providing you're not a pussy."

"Mark me down as a pussy," Tree said.

"No surprise there," Slippery muttered.

"Slippery," Ferne said in a warning voice, "cut it out."

Slippery muttered some more.

"Slippery's got a point, Tree," Ferne said. "The problem with sitting around waiting for something to happen, that's when nothing happens. You got to make things happen."

Tree's cell phone rang. "Edith Goldman" appeared on the read-out. "What is it, Edith?" Tree said into the phone.

"Where are you?" Short and snappy.

"What difference does it make?"

"Detective Markfield is looking for you."

"Do you know what he wants?"

"I'm not certain, but given recent events, he may want to arrest you for murder."

Tree didn't say anything.

"Are you there?" said Edith Goldman.

"I'm here."

"You've got twenty-four hours to appear at police headquarters."

"Or?"

"I presume they would issue an arrest warrant for you."

"Okay."

"Tree, this is very serious."

"I know it is, Edith."

Through the windshield Tree could see Sasha in a black suit emerge from the building and stop to light a cigarette.

"Edith, I've got to go."

"Tree—"

He closed his cell phone.

"To hell with this," Slippery said. Before Ferne could stop him, he leapt out of the van and charged toward Sasha.

"What's he doing?"

"With Slippery you never know," Ferne said.

Tree watched with growing consternation as Slippery reached Sasha, grabbed his shoulder, and spun him around. Sasha reacted by promptly kicking Slippery between the legs. Slippery cried out as he hit the ground.

Sasha was fumbling under his jacket for what Tree imagined was a gun, when Slippery pulled up his pant leg to reveal a black leather ankle holster. The next thing he had a straight razor in his hand, slashing at Sasha's calf. Sasha screamed and fell away as Ferne jumped from the van, baseball bat in hand.

Sasha was on his knees holding his bleeding leg still trying to get to his gun when Ferne swung the bat across his skull with an ugly crack. The gun clattered to the pavement.

She was about to hit him again when Tree lurched out of the van hollering, "Ferne, don't!"

Ferne hesitated, the bat upraised.

"That's enough," Tree called out.

Slippery was on his feet, holding the razor, his face twisted, yelling, *"I'm gonna slice him in two, I'm gonna slice the bastard in two!"*

He waved the razor around but otherwise did not move to carry out his threat. Ferne, meanwhile, dropped the bat, lifted Sasha up, and hauled him over to the van. She opened the back doors and flung him inside.

"Tree," she called, "grab my bat will you? And pick up Sasha's gun. Slippery, come on, let's go. I need you behind the wheel."

"He kicked my package," Slippery cried. "You see that? He kicked my package. I'm gonna slice him in half for that."

"Slice him later. Right now, we've got to get out of here." Ferne slammed the van doors closed.

Tree grabbed the bat and retrieved the gun, a Glock pistol. Slippery replaced the razor in its ankle sheath. He suddenly lunged forward so that his unshaven face hovered beneath Tree's chin. "You think I don't know what you're up to?"

"What am I up to, Slippery?"

"You think I don't see how you're leading her on? You're a married man. You ought to be ashamed of yourself."

Tree shook his head. "You've got to be kidding."

"I'm the one who would go to the wall for that woman," Slippery said. "I'm the one who can make her happy. Not you, pal. Not by a mile."

"Slippery, I think you've got the wrong idea."

"Want to know what the worst day of my life was? The worst day was when that gun didn't go off and blow a hole right through your stinking guts."

Slippery hobbled away to the van leaving Tree bewildered. He held the baseball bat in one hand, Sasha's Glock in the other, a real tough guy, the rival to Bailey Street, wannabe killer and lovesick romantic.

"Tree," Ferne yelled. "Let's go!"

Slippery had the van started by the time Tree got inside. Ferne was on her knees at the back raising Sasha into a sitting position. He was groggy and pale. A thin red line trickled out of his ear and down his chin. Blood seeped from his slashed calf. He did not look in great shape.

"He's all right," Ferne said. She braced Sasha against the van's wall. "Aren't you Sasha?"

Sasha's eyes flickered, and he let out a groan.

"There you go," Ferne said. "Sasha's right as rain and anxious to help out. What do you want to know, Tree?"

"Where I can find Aksel Baldur."

"You hear that, Sasha? My friend wants to know Aksel's location."

Sasha looked at her with uncomprehending eyes. Ferne shook him. "Sasha? Are you listening to me? We're going to drop you off at the hospital just as soon as you tell us what we want to know."

Tree thought he heard Sasha say something like, "Supposed to take the car ..."

"What was that, Sasha?" Ferne said.

Sasha said in a louder voice, "Supposed to take the car over to the house."

"Aksel's at the house?"

Sasha moved his head up and down.

36

Tree found a set of keys in Sasha's pocket and used them to get into his second floor office. He found another black suit that more or less fit, along with a tie and a peaked cap. He got into the suit and then went back downstairs and outside to where Ferne leaned against the van. Slippery remained unhappily at his post behind the wheel.

"Sasha's looking a little worse for wear," Ferne said. "I think we'd better drop him off at the hospital."

"What are you going to tell them?"

"Not going to tell them anything. We just leave him outside Emergency. They'll find him soon enough and take care of him. The thing is, Tree, are you going to be all right on your own?"

"As long as you're coming back," Tree said.

"Exactly what is it you're trying to accomplish here, Tree?" Ferne spoke as if she was conducting a job interview.

"I don't know. But I think Baldur may have killed my daughter-in-law. Somehow, I've got to get closer to him, find out more. Maybe I'm going about it the wrong way. Maybe I should go to the police."

"Where I come from," Ferne said, "it's never a very good idea to get the police involved. Better to settle these things on your own terms. As soon as I drop off our pal Sasha, I'll be back, and then we'll see what we can shake out of Mr. Baldur. In the meantime, keep your cell phone handy. I'll do the same."

"Thanks, Ferne," Tree said. "I really appreciate this. Incidentally, I finally figured out why Slippery doesn't like me."

"Detective Tree at work," Ferne said with a grin.

"He needs reassurance that there is nothing going on between us."

"But there is something between us."

"Ferne."

She shrugged. "Slippery's in love with me. The trouble is, I'm not in love with him. Funny world, huh? I love you, you don't love me. Slippery loves me, but I don't love him. You two don't like each other. Nonetheless, here we are all thrown together in a green van with a gun and a baseball bat and a guy bleeding."

"I just don't want trouble with Slippery."

"He thinks you're a wuss."

"I *am* a wuss," Tree said.

Ferne laughed and handed Tree Sasha's Glock.

"What's this?"

"Evidence you're not a wuss anymore," Ferne said.

———

The vanity license plate on Sasha's Lincoln read "FLAWILD." That was Tree all right. FLAWILD. He got into the car. The interior smelled new. He opened the glove compartment and found a pair of dark glasses and put them on.

He studied himself in the rearview mirror, feeling more confident viewing the world through tinted lenses. Even so, moments later his heart was in his mouth as he turned the Lincoln through the iron gates into Aksel Baldur's estate. Sasha's Glock was a discomfiting presence against his waist. His cell phone jumped on the passenger seat beside him.

Ferne said, "We just deposited the package at the hospital." Meaning, the unwell Sasha. "Where are you?"

"Just coming in the gates," Tree said.

"Okay. We're on our way over there."

Tree thought he could hear Slippery's complaining voice in the background.

"Everything all right?"

"Everything is hunky-dory. Just be careful."

Tree swung the car along the drive up to the main entrance. He came to a stop, took a deep breath, and told himself to relax. He was about to get out of the car when a figure came out of the house. Tree fumbled with the electric window switch on the driver side door. The back window uttered an electronic gasp and started down. He tried again and this time the front window rolled down as a hard face dropped into view.

Tony Dodge said, "Where's Sasha?"

"He's sick. Started to throw up. I just dropped him off at the hospital. He sent me to pick up Mr. Baldur."

Dodge wore a soft gray Armani suit that almost made you forget he had just been released from prison.

Almost.

He gave Tree another of the scowls that had probably scared everyone on his cellblock.

"Park around the back and then come inside."

Tree nodded and started forward along the drive. A delivery van was parked at the back but otherwise the lot was empty today.

The enormous house loomed silently above him as he exited the car and debated what to do about the Glock. He decided to hide it under the front seat. Once this was done, he locked the car, made sure his cell phone was in his side pocket, and adjusted his sunglasses before heading to the rear entrance.

He knocked a couple of times. When no one answered, he opened the door and stepped into a gleaming kitchen, camera-ready for the Food Network.

A tiny maid in a crisp blue uniform appeared. "Where's Sasha?" she asked.

"Sick," Tree said.

"Sick with what?" The maid opened the door of a stainless steel refrigerator you could park a car in.

"I don't know," Tree said. "He was throwing up. I took him to the hospital."

"That guy," the maid said. "That guy don't take care of himself. He smoke. It's gonna kill him."

"Bad habit," Tree said.

The maid withdrew a pitcher of freshly squeezed orange juice and took it over to a marble counter. She set it down and then retrieved a glass from the cupboard above the counter.

"You hungry?" She poured orange juice into the glass. "You want something to eat?"

"No, I'm fine thanks."

She shrugged. "Up to you."

Aksel Baldur strolled in, holding an iPhone against his ear. He wore a loose white linen shirt open at the neck to show off the medallion dangling from a gold necklace.

"Circus of Life." He chuckled into the iPhone. "Nice ring to it, don't you think? Fashion, baby. It's all played out against the circus of life."

Baldur stopped when he saw Tree but continued to speak into the phone. "Of course they're gonna be there. How can life be a circus if you don't have chickies under the big top? Yeah, right. That's all you come for. All the cute little babies with their flat tummies and their perky titties. You don't even look at the clothes. Sure, sure. See you tonight, amigo."

Baldur closed the iPhone. The maid handed him the glass of orange juice. He said, "Thanks, Rosa." To Tree: "Who are you?"

The maid said, "Sasha's sick. He sent this guy instead."

"I don't like this," Baldur said. He placed the orange juice on the counter.

Rosa frowned. "You no want the orange juice?"

Baldur's tadpole eyes focused on Tree. "Sasha doesn't show up so he just sends whoever happens to be standing around?"

"Sasha's gone to the hospital," Rosa said. "And you never drink the orange juice I squeeze for you."

"The hospital?" Baldur looked at Tree. "What's wrong with him?"

Tree shrugged. "He was throwing up. I took him over to Emergency. I wanted to stay with him, but he said he'd be okay, to get over here."

Tony Dodge entered the kitchen. Baldur turned to him. "You hear this about Sasha?"

"Just now," Dodge said. "I tried to get him on his cell, but there's no answer."

"You know this guy?" said Baldur.

Tony Dodge looked Tree up and down and shrugged. "I never know who Sasha's got on the go."

Baldur looked at Tree again. "What's your name?"

"Eddie," Tree said. Did he look like an Eddie?

"Okay, Eddie," Baldur said, "I've got a couple more calls to make. You bring the car around to the front. I'll meet you there."

"Yes, sir," Tree said.

Feeling as though he had passed some sort of test, Tree went out to the parking lot and got into the car. Baldur was waiting at the front by the time he drove around. Tree hopped out and opened the rear door for him. Baldur was already poking out another number on his phone as he slipped inside.

By the time Tree got behind the wheel, Baldur was saying into the iPhone, "Tell him that if he doesn't do something about the price, I'll move my business to Vietnam. Tell him I can do much better there, and they don't screw around. All of which is true, incidentally."

He paused to listen before going on: "No, but I'm getting real tired of these creeps jerking me around. I've got better things to do than sit in Shanghai waiting on a bunch of morons. Okay, get back to me as soon as you know."

"Hey." In the rear view mirror Tree could see Baldur's florid face darken. "So what are we doing sitting here?"

"I need to know where we're going, Mr. Baldur."

"We're going over to the Ringling Museum," Baldur said. "Where do you think we're going?"

37

By the time John Ringling moved the winter headquarters of the Ringling circus empire to Florida in 1927, his four brothers had died, and John was left to run the show by himself.

A couple of years later, John Ringling owned virtually every circus in America and was one of the world's richest men. Not surprisingly, he had no qualms about lavishing a considerable fortune on the creation of a thirty-room Sarasota mansion inspired by the palazzos he and his wife had visited in Venice. These days, only the state could keep up such lavish digs, and thus the John and Mable Ringling Museum of Art was open to a public anxious to see how John and Mable had lived and view what they had collected.

As Tree drove the Lincoln along North Tamiami Trail, Baldur issued an angry expletive and threw his iPhone on the seat. Tree glanced into the rear view mirror and caught Baldur staring at him.

"Everything okay, Mr. Baldur?"

"Eddie? Is that your name?"

"That's right, Mr. Baldur."

"Where you from, Eddie?"

"Lot of places," Tree said. "Chicago, originally."

"Chicago? I live in Chicago."

"Is that right? You're not from down here?"

"Eddie, do I sound like I'm from down here?" With a tinge of disdain—apparently his preferred tone with inferiors.

"You don't sound as though you're from Chicago, either."

"Where does it sound like I'm from?" Baldur had adopted a slightly amused expression.

"I don't know," Tree said. "One of the Scandinavian countries? Norway? Sweden?"

Baldur waved a dismissive hand. "No, no. Finland. Not Scandinavian, although that's what most Americans think. Finland is a Nordic country, not a Scandinavian country."

"I stand corrected," Tree said.

"Everyone makes the same mistake."

The GPS told Tree to turn right onto Ringling Plaza. With relief, he spotted the complex ahead. Baldur had his iPhone in hand again, punching out another number. When he got someone's answering machine, he hung up in disgust, and then leaned forward as Tree drove through the entranceway.

"Park close to the mansion."

"Yes sir."

Tree guided the Lincoln along the main drive past the Circus Museum and the Banyan Café. To his left, he could see an impressive rose garden before the road arched in a circle to the mansion entrance.

As soon as Tree stopped the car, Baldur jumped out, calling, "Follow me."

The boss was being unexpectedly friendly, Tree thought as he got out and joined Baldur on the walkway in front of the house. The breeze blew Baldur's blond hair back and made his white shirt billow. He looked like a galleon setting sail as he watched workers erect billboards announcing "Life Is a Circus." A crane lifted a huge cutout of a smiling Aksel Baldur off a flatbed truck. Searchlights were mounted into position atop webs of scaffolding on either side of the drive.

Baldur turned to study the mansion façade, a picture book combination of Arabian Nights fantasy and Venetian palazzo, anchored by an impressive tower of terra cotta and stucco.

"I love this place," he said. "You been here before, Eddie?"

"A couple of years ago," Tree said.

"Ca' d'Zan," Baldur said. "That's what Ringling called his home. Supposedly it means House of John in the Venetian dialect. There are fifty-six rooms in Ca' d'Zan. Ringling and Mabel filled them all with something like ten thousand pieces of art and antiques they collected in Europe."

"How do you do that?" Tree said. "How do you find ten thousand pieces of anything that you want that badly?"

Baldur smiled again. "See, Eddie? That's why you're always going to be doing the driving, instead of being driven. John and Mabel didn't think small. They couldn't stop acquiring things; too much was never enough for them.

"John Ringling was the king of the circus," Baldur continued. "He owned his own railroad that transported the greatest show on earth across the country each season. Thousands of men and women and animals. The Ringling Circus would arrive in town, offload the cars, set up tents, feed everyone, do a show, take it all down again, put it back on the train and be off to the next town, all in twenty-four hours. Night after night they did this. No computers, almost no communications. Manpower and organization made it work. Ringling was something else. He lived like a king and then lost everything and died with three hundred dollars in his bank account."

"That's how you want to end up?" Tree asked.

Baldur gave him a wide smile. "A little more than three hundred dollars—maybe. Rich guys like Ringling, they are my heroes. My role models. Larger than life. Outsized appetites. Always greedy for more."

He started walking toward the house. "When I grew up we had nothing. My old man was a monster. I should not have been able to survive him, but I did and look at me now.

"So I live fast and hard, Eddie, just like John Ringling. Full out. Get everything, lose it, get it back again. That's me, that's what I like to do. Who knows how it will turn out? Bad, I suppose. No reason to think it won't. In the meantime, it's a hell of a ride."

As he finished, Tree noticed that the huge Aksel cutout had been successfully lowered into place. It didn't quite dwarf the nearby Royal Palms. Someone must have miscalculated. Baldur studied the gigantic reproduction of himself. His eyes took on a dreamy expression.

"What do you think, Eddie? Impressive, huh? We're presenting my fall collection tonight. You see yourself up there like that and you think, okay, all the crap you have to go through, it's worth it."

"Looks like it's going to be quite a show."

"Not just a show, Eddie. An *extravaganza!*"

Aksel the showman strode up the steps to the mansion entrance. Tree hurried to keep up.

Inside, a red-carpeted foyer opened through a series of archways onto a two-story atrium surrounding a gloomy sitting room full of heavy, ornate furniture. The gloom soon would be broken by the lights being hung from the balconies. Workmen removed the furniture to make space for the runway being laid the length of the room. Others unfolded stacked chairs and placed them on either side of the runway.

"Hang in for a few minutes, Eddie," Baldur said.

He crossed the room and disappeared around the corner. As soon as he was gone, Tree fished out his cell and called Ferne's number. It immediately went to voicemail.

"It's just me, Ferne," Tree said. "I'm with Baldur at the Ringling Museum. Get over here as soon as you can."

He closed the cell. Six jean-clad young women, stick thin, wandered through the mounting chaos. Two of them gingerly stepped onto the runway. Tree's cell phone rang. He looked at the readout. It was Ferne.

"Did you get my message?" Tree said.

Whoever was on the other end of the phone did not respond.

"Ferne?"

The phone went dead.

A cold fear pricked at his spine. He sensed something behind him and turned. Baldur said, "What are you doing standing there?"

"Waiting for you," Tree said.

"Let's get going."

"Yes, sir. Where are we headed?"

"Back to the house."

In the car, Baldur busied himself texting on the iPhone. He didn't speak to Tree until they pulled into the driveway. "Swing around to the back and drop me there," he ordered.

Tree guided the car around to the rear and came to a stop.

"Will there be anything else, Mr. Baldur?"

He looked at the rear view mirror. Baldur was staring at him.

"Just get the door open for me."

Tree opened the driver's door and stepped out. He opened the passenger door to allow Baldur to exit. Tony Dodge appeared with Fudd and Elmer. Baldur gave Tree a dead-eyed smile. "Did you know we've got Jay and the Americans performing tonight?"

"Jay and the Americans?" Tree said.

"You like them?"

"Didn't know they were still around."

"I love their music. 'Young Girl?'" He grinned. "It's practically my theme song."

"No kidding," Tree said.

Aksel took the smile off his face. "How stupid do you think I am, Mr. Callister? You don't think I watch the TV news and know what you look like?"

Tree found he was having trouble swallowing.

Baldur said, "Tell me what you are doing here."

"I suppose I'd like to find out how you're involved with Elizabeth Traven, and why you would kill Kendra Callister."

Baldur's eyes became smaller and blacker. "Yes, Jay and the Americans are going to be great. But I'm afraid you're not going to be there to see them."

38

As Baldur turned away, Fudd stepped smartly forward. His face was still swollen, Tree observed, just before Fudd swung him around and then yanked his arms behind him. He felt cold steel enveloping his wrists, the rotating arms of handcuffs ratcheted so tight they hurt.

Next, Elmer, assisted by Fudd, hustled Tree over to where a lime green van was parked. Ferne's van, he thought dimly.

As soon as the back doors opened, he was picked up and tossed inside onto a plastic sheet that held an unmoving body.

He stared into Ferne Clowers' dead eyes.

He reeled away in horror, the plastic slippery and crackling. The doors slammed closed. In the semidarkness, he twisted around on the sheet coming face to face with the corpse of Slippery Street.

Then he realized what was making the plastic sheet so wet and sticky—it was drenched in blood from the two bodies.

He heard more doors slamming and the van starting up. It lurched forward, tossing him against Ferne's body. Ferne who loved him even though she tried to kill him; Ferne who promised to be his guardian angel, who would watch his back—the promise broken by the murderous Fudd and Elmer. You came at them with a baseball bat, they retaliated by killing you.

The van picked up speed. The bodies shifted against him. He tried to concentrate on things that might come in handy later; the state of the roads they traveled; the sounds outside; the time elapsed.

But the state of the roads seemed smooth enough, providing no indication where they were headed. As for outside sounds, there were none. Just the soothing hum of the engine and the rush of air as the van rumbled across an unseen landscape. Any sense of elapsed time eluded him. But then what difference did it make? Even if he was able to draw conclusions, what use were they? The van would come to a stop, the back doors would open, and they would kill him. If he had any doubts as to the outcome, he had only to consider his traveling companions.

The van slowed to make a sharp turn onto rough road. It shook and bumped along for a few minutes and then came to an abrupt stop.

Silence.

The back doors opened. Fudd and Elmer reached in and pulled him out of the van, dropping him face down on spongy ground. The two thugs loomed above him. The fading light bounced off the lenses of Fudd's glasses so that it looked like his eyes were on fire.

"What did you think, Tree?" he said. "You think you could send that supersized freak in a dress around with her baseball bat and her skanky little tool of a buddy and you'd be okay?"

"He's even dumber than he looks," Elmer said.

"And right now he looks pretty dumb to me," Fudd said.

Elmer went out of view, and then the bodies of Ferne and Slippery landed with dull thuds beside him.

Fudd said, "Mr. Baldur told us not to kill you. Okay, we're not going to kill you."

"Nope," chorused Fudd. "We are going to follow orders. Someone tells us not to kill someone, we don't do it."

"No we don't," Elmer said, lifting his foot to kick Tree in the face. Tree groaned and spat out blood and teeth.

Then his hands were being lifted so that the handcuffs could be removed from his wrists. Merciful relief—but only for a moment. Either Fudd or Elmer—he couldn't tell who— grabbed his right arm and reattached a handcuff to his wrist. Then the other arm and another handcuff.

The damp ground cushioned him like a soft bed, dulling the pain drilling through his body. He would lie like this for a while and then he would figure the way out. There had to be a way, all it took was him closing his eyes for a few minutes. Then he could figure it out.

39

He regained something like consciousness, floating in a black void where uncertain shapes formed and re-formed before dropping into focus: Ferne Clowers' bloody body on one side of him, Slippery's on the other; an impressive barrier of mangrove; two alligators.

The alligators required more concentration. Yes, they were alligators all right, approximately twenty yards away. He tried to move, and that's when he discovered that his left wrist was attached to the dead Ferne.

When he tried to shift his right hand, it proved equally difficult since it was tethered to Slippery. So that was it. He was lost in a Grimm's fairy tale forest, handcuffed to two corpses as a couple of alligators closed in.

Not good, he thought.

He spat out a wad of mucus and blood in order to clear his clogged mouth. Immediately, he regretted the impulse—the two alligators were certain to regard Tree's blood as an invitation. Wasn't this feeding time for creatures of the wild? He had seen something about that on the Discovery Channel.

The alligators moved suddenly, with a speed that caught Tree by surprise. Weren't gators slow-moving creatures? No, that was the point. They *seemed* slow moving, he remembered reading. But in fact they weren't, particularly when food was involved.

Tree sat up as best he could and began jerking his arms up and down. Slippery, lighter in death, moved around like a puppet on a string. But Ferne was the immovable whale. Not that his movements made much difference. The alligators appeared unimpressed.

The bigger of the two moved again, jaws snapping closed around Ferne's immense torso. Flesh ripped away in a spray of blood and torn bone. The alligator dived back into the shadows as if afraid his partner might attempt to rob him of his dinner.

The second alligator had other ideas, launching its own lightning strike into Ferne's torso. The force of the creature's tearing jaws slammed Tree forward. Then the gator disappeared with its dinner.

Tree shook with fear. Soon the alligators would return for more, and it would not be long before they got to him. Frantically, he tried to crawl away, but the bodies were so much dead weight holding him in place.

The last glimmers of daylight squeezed through the dense mangroves. In minutes, the world would be in darkness. Tree saw Slippery's bared leg and the leather sheath strapped to his ankle. The gleaming stainless steel handle of Slippery's straight razor was just visible. Tree lunged for it.

And could not reach the razor.

He tried one more time, but that only brought more agony. He rested a bit before pulling Ferne closer to him so that he had more leverage to reach Slippery. Yes, that was better, he thought. Not as much pain. He bent slowly forward, reaching out, and now his fingers brushed the razor handle.

He straightened, took a deep breath, and then bent over, straining further forward, willing his body to become longer.

And it worked.

Somehow, he had the handle in his grasp, sliding it out of Slippery's ankle sheath.

He straightened, holding the razor. Tree used his teeth to pull the blade from the handle. Could he do this? Did he have it in him?

As though reading his mind, one of the alligators reappeared through the gloom, having finished the first course. What he had to do abruptly became much more doable.

He shifted around to Ferne's body, lifted her cold hand, and put the blade against her wrist.

He closed his eyes, gritted his teeth, and went to work.

40

Tree Callister running—not running exactly, more like stumbling, lurching, trying not to scream with every tortured footfall, trying to choke down a rekindled sense of panic borne of the knowledge that he had no idea where he was. He thought Fudd and Elmer had driven him along an unpaved roadway. But in the dark he could not find any road. He could barely see his hand in front of him. He tried not to consider the handcuff dangling from his right wrist let alone the matching handcuff attached to his left.

Furthermore, he did not want to think about what he had just forced himself to do in order to free himself from Ferne and Slippery; what he'd done so he would not become alligator food. He did not wish to contemplate what those alligators were currently doing to what was left of the bodies. Ferne did not love Slippery who loved Ferne. Now they were together forever. Maybe that would finally make Slippery happy. He was not so certain about Ferne.

The drifting moon squeezed out from behind thick clouds, illuminating a darkly shadowed hell that in daylight would be forest but at this time of night was an impenetrable tangle.

An exposed tree root sent him sprawling to the ground. Agony.

On his knees, he raised his arms and screamed and screamed, his screams echoing through the primordial forest. He lay there exhausted for a time, feeling the warmth of tears running down his cheeks. What would Ferne think of him sobbing like a baby in the middle of the woods? Ferne who loved him unconditionally; Ferne who would die for him; Ferne, who, if he was being honest, made his skin crawl.

She might gently point out that it didn't matter what Tree thought, she loved him, anyway. And as for the crying, that wasn't going to help things. Ferne would be right.

He got to his feet and started off again.

An hour or so later—it could have been longer, shorter, he had no real sense of time—Tree found himself at the edge of a body of water. He sank to the ground, unable to go further and uncertain where he would go even if he could. He was lost in the dark.

After he had lain on the ground for a while, a light flashed in the distance. Was he seeing things?

No, it was a light, and it was moving toward him. Sound accompanied light—an outboard motor?

A small boat came into view, a running light at its stern. Tree could make out the outline of a man in a baseball cap. He called out to him. The man cut the engine. "What's that?" he said.

"Hey," Tree said.

"Hey, yourself," returned the man in the boat.

"I'm in trouble," Tree said.

The man turned the boat toward shore and shouted, "No doubt you are, being out here in the middle of nowhere."

"Where am I?" Tree said.

"Myakka State Park. The question I have is this: if you don't know where you are, how the blazes did you get here?"

"Car ran off the road," Tree said. "I banged myself up, sort of got disoriented in the dark and ended up here."

The boat's prow scraped along the shallow bottom and held. A flashlight beam cut the darkness, illuminating Tree. "You do look the worse for wear, fella," the man said.

"Can you help me out?" Tree said.

"Well, if I don't help you, you truly are up the creek without a paddle," the man said amiably. "Push off the boat, and then jump in. I'll get you down to the marina."

"There's a marina?"

"Sure. Not far from here."

Tree leaned forward, grabbing the bow and shoving at it until the boat came unstuck from the bottom. He hopped in, letting out a yelp of pain.

"You okay, fella?"

"I'm hurting a bit," Tree admitted.

"I've got my truck at the marina. I can drive you to a hospital."

"I really appreciate this."

"Earl Tompkins," the man said, leaning forward to shake Tree's hand. Under the baseball cap a weathered face had eluded a razor for a week.

"Tree Callister. What are you doing out here, Earl?"

"What folks usually do out here. Either they fish or they run away from the world. I guess I do a little of both."

"Well, I'm sure glad you're here, Earl."

"What I can't figure, Tree, is how you got so far into the park. The highway is miles away."

"I sort of blacked out," Tree said.

"Whatever happened, you are one lucky man."

"Didn't seem like it for a while there, Earl, but I guess I am at that."

Earl Tompkins put the throttle into reverse, backing the boat away from the shore.

"Say," he said, "what's that hanging from your wrist?"

41

You might say I'm indulging in a little criminal behavior myself tonight," Earl said. His way, Tree supposed, of reconciling the fact that his passenger had handcuffs attached to both wrists.

"I thought you were fishing," Tree said.

"I said I was fishing, didn't I? I said that because I didn't want you to know what I was really doing."

"What were you really doing?"

Earl grinned and said, "Fishing."

Tree managed a grin right back. "Okay, Earl. Fishing it is." Wondering what Earl might be up to that was illegal.

"You wanted by law enforcement, Tree?"

"No, I'm not that serious a bad guy," Tree said.

"They put two pairs of handcuffs on you, I dunno, seems to me that's pretty serious."

"The handcuffs were a misunderstanding," Tree said.

Earl burst out laughing. "That's some misunderstanding, Tree."

"A couple of fellows got the wrong idea about me, that's all."

Earl laughed some more but did not pursue the matter. A darkened marina came into view. Earl slipped the throttle into neutral and maneuvered the boat against the dock. He hopped out and tied off, then leaned down and offered a hand to help Tree up and out. Tree tumbled onto the dock, reawakening the pain in his side. He groaned and tried to catch his breath.

"You all right, Tree?" Earl asked.

"I just need a minute," Tree said.

Earl lowered himself to his haunches close to where Tree lay. "The thing is, you need help, and I aim to provide it. But then if you really are a wanted fella, I suspect there might be some sort of reward out for you."

"No, Earl," Tree said. "I'm afraid there's no reward for me."

"Even so, you wouldn't want me turning you over to the law enforcement now would you?"

Tree looked up at him. The fisherman's grizzled face contained a certain craft Tree had failed to spot. "What is it, Earl?"

"You know how it is, a life of crime out here just ain't all that rewarding. So I guess I'd like you to help me out a bit. I scratch your back, you scratch mine type of thing."

"You want me to scratch your back, Earl?"

"Why don't you just give me some money?"

Tree thought about this for a time and then said, "Sure, Earl. I don't mind helping out a fellow crook. Let me see what I've got."

He reached into his pocket and pulled out Slippery's razor. He flicked the blade out and grabbed the front of Earl's jacket with one hand, and with the other pressed the edge of the blade against Earl's throat.

"Hey, take it easy," Earl said in a strangled voice.

"Listen to me carefully, Earl. I've done some things tonight I've never done before, okay? So if I have to slit your throat on top of everything else, well, I'm pretty sure I would do it. Do you understand?"

Earl nodded slowly. "Hey, no use anyone getting hurt, Tree."

Tree eased himself up, holding the blade firmly against Earl's unshaven throat. "What I want you to do, I want you to reach into your pocket and pull out your keys."

"You're not going to take my truck, are you Tree?"

"Yes, I am, Earl. But in return I'm not going to cut your throat. That's a pretty good tradeoff if you ask me."

"You have a point there, Tree. You have a point."

Earl eased his hand into his jeans pockets and fished out a transponder key attached to a key ring shaped like a teddy bear. He handed it to Tree. "What they call a PATS key. Stands for Passive Anti-Theft System. So's no one can steal your truck."

"That's great, Earl. Glad you've got the latest anti-theft devices. I'll feel much safer driving the truck now."

"I wish you wouldn't take my truck," Earl said in a plaintive voice. "It's brand new. That's theft, you know."

"I'm not stealing it, Earl. I'm borrowing it. You give me your phone number and when I get to where I'm going, I'll call you and you can come and get it."

"There's a bit of trouble with that truck," Earl said hesitantly.

"What kind of trouble?"

"Well, sir, it's stolen."

"Stolen? Who stole it?"

"I did."

Tree broke into a grin. "There you go, Earl. Couple of bad guys like us, helping one another. Honor among thieves, that's what it is."

"From what I know of thieves, there ain't much honor," Earl said sullenly.

"Then it's like you pointed out. Me being such a dangerous criminal, theft isn't much of anything. Wouldn't even give it a second thought. You don't want to know what I was doing out there in the swamp. So you certainly don't want to get in my way when I take your truck."

"No," Earl said, the fear burning bright in his eyes.

Good, Tree thought. Someone in the world was actually afraid of him.

Practice for what was to come.

42

The host of the phone-in show on the impressive radio in Earl's bright red Ford Ranger said there was indisputable evidence that the U.S. Government faked the Apollo moon landings.

The filmmaker Stanley Kubrick had conspired with NASA and used outtakes from his 1968 masterpiece, *2001: A Space Odyssey*, to make it *look* as though America landed on the moon when, in fact, no such landing took place.

Few callers disagreed with the proposition. That would certainly make Fudd happy. All sorts of people out there in radio land shared his conspiracy-minded view of things.

Tree fiddled with the dial. Late night Florida radio was full of talk show nut cases and cheating country music women. The evangelists waited in the wings. He chose country music over the nuts—achy-breaky, making him think of Freddie. He thought of how much he loved her and how far away she seemed. He thought of his son, even further away—on the moon where the Apollo astronauts never landed.

He thought about what he was planning to do. Not much of a plan, he admitted to himself. A patchwork of irrational notions, maybe, but hardly a plan. Freddie would think he was out of his mind, and she would be right. The women in his life always were right; invariably, therefore, he was wrong. He wondered why that hard fact never stopped him.

It should have. But it didn't.

He came along Bay Shore Road, past the arched entranceway to the John and Mable Ringling Museum. Searchlights crisscrossed the sky—Aksel Baldur letting the world know he was having a party. Put on your tight dress, baby, get out that phony ID, and prepare to meet dirty old rich men.

The traffic around the museum slowed him until he turned the corner, and the world became abruptly silent. Tree pulled over onto the shoulder and got out of the truck, stiff and sore, everything aching anew.

He limped through a stand of trees and found himself on the museum grounds. He crossed a roadway separating the trees from the elegant gallery that housed the Ringlings' massive art collection. He came around the building onto a vast swatch of lawn, past the terraced center courtyard filled with examples of the statuary John and Mable had picked up during their European sojourns.

Beyond the courtyard, a penumbra of light marked the Circus of Life spectacularly unfolding along the walkway to Ca' d'Zan, John and Mabel Ringling's labor of domestic love. Tree didn't go toward the lights, though. Instead, he veered away from the crowds he could see along the walkway, skirted the rose garden, crossing wooded grounds until he reached a parking area created for the vehicles that had transported Axel Baldur's particularly important guests.

The sound of Jay and the Americans singing "Cara Mia" carried out of the mansion as Tree moved along the limos, looking at license plates. The Lincoln bearing the vanity license plate FLAWILD was parked at the end. Now, Tree thought, now if only the door was unlocked. And it was. He reached under the driver's seat, and his hand closed around the Glock pistol.

Exactly where he had left it.

He reclosed the driver's door and stood in the night holding the Glock. Jay and the Americans warbled in the background. The warm breeze rose off the nearby water. He felt better holding the gun. He hated himself for thinking like that. But the gun provided the confidence he required.

Shoving the gun into his belt, he made his way to the promenade adjacent to Ca' d'Zan overlooking Sarasota Bay. Beautifully dressed guests wreathed in smoke huddled near the entrance beyond the promenade. Tree watched from the shadows. One of the smokers separated from the others and started away. Tony Dodge tossed what was left of his cigarette and walked straight for Tree.

He waited until Dodge reached the trees before he came up behind him, jamming the Glock against the back of his ear. Dodge jerked in surprise. Tree put a hand on a powerful shoulder and brought him to a stop.

"Hey, Tony," Tree said in as calm a voice as he could muster. "How's the party?"

"What the hell are you doing here?"

"Didn't I mention it? I'm a huge Jay and the Americans fan."

Tree patted him down, keeping his Glock against Dodge's ear. He reached inside his suit jacket to retrieve a gun from a shoulder holster. Tree backed off a couple of paces testing the weight of Dodge's gun. It nestled nicely in the palm of his hand. "What is this?"

Dodge turned to face Tree, taking note of his sorry state. He nodded at the gun. "Walther PPK," he said carefully. "The James Bond gun. My pride and joy, so why don't you give it back to me, and then get out of here?"

Tree pointed the Walther at him. "Let's go for a ride."

"You read too many detective novels, man," Dodge said. "I'm not going anywhere."

"Yes, you are." Trying to sound as though he meant it. Dodge was wrong. He didn't read *enough* detective novels. Otherwise, he might be a little more certain about how to pull off the tough guy act.

Dodge's smirk widened. "What do you think you're gonna do, Tree? Shoot me in front of all these well-dressed folks?"

The adrenalin pumped through him, a river of energy that, despite his exhausted state, allowed him to think he could get away with anything, even smashing a gun into the head of a well-muscled ex-con who could probably eat him for breakfast under normal circumstances.

Dodge staggered back. The smirk disappeared.

Tree hit him again. Dodge's nose exploded in blood. He sank to the ground. Tree waved the gun at him and said, "Get up."

This time, Dodge did as he was told, wobbly, managing to get to his feet while holding his shattered nose. Inside Ca' d'Zan, Jay and the Americans sang "Young Girl," Baldur's favorite song. Tree pushed Dodge toward the parking lot.

When they reached the FLAWILD Lincoln, Dodge leaned against the side.

"In the car, Tony," Tree said.

"Don't have the key," Dodge said.

"Yes, you do. Now get it out."

Dodge looked at Tree and then fished the key out of his pocket.

"Get inside," Tree ordered.

Dodge opened the door and squeezed behind the wheel. Tree stepped back to the rear, and got into the car, keeping the Glock trained on Dodge.

When the Lincoln growled to life, Tree said, "Drive to Baldur's place."

He could see Dodge glance at him in the rear view mirror. "You know, you're smart enough to somehow be alive, don't be so dumb as to stick around."

"Drive, Tony," Tree said.

"You're a dead man, pal."

Tree did not respond, not sure Dodge wasn't right.

43

Let me try this on you," Tree said as Tony Dodge drove through the Sarasota night. "Brand Traven discovered his wife was involved with a group that specialized in high-end sex trafficking, bringing young women in from Mexico and Latin America, providing the right kind of available women for a certain kind of rich clientele."

As he talked, Tree kept the snout of the Glock pressed against Dodge's neck.

"The Red Rose sex trade solved Elizabeth Traven's financial problems and then some. But Traven was appalled when she told him what she was doing—appalled and furious. So furious, in fact, that he got hold of a professional killer he had met in prison who was just about to be released. He hired him to take care of his wife. Only the wife got to the killer, offering a better deal. So the killer hooks up with Elizabeth Traven and the next thing, Brand Traven is dead."

The ex-con remained silent. Tree couldn't see his face, and had no sense of how he was reacting.

"Elizabeth probably hired me to help her with an alibi," Tree went on. "To a certain extent, she was telling the truth—her husband had planned to kill her. It's just that she got there first.

"And maybe Elizabeth's subsequent arrest was even anticipated, knowing that in the end she wouldn't be convicted because she did not murder her husband. Meanwhile, the killer went to work for Elizabeth's associate, Aksel Baldur. When Baldur decided that he didn't like the way Kendra Callister deceived him, there you were, Tony, to take care of her, just like you took care of Brand Traven."

That drew a derisive snort from Dodge. "You should be writing fiction, man. You got yourself a vivid imagination. But that's all it is. Nowhere close to the truth."

"I like the story, Tony. Why don't we try it out on the police?"

"Sure, man. You try anything you want. That don't make it true."

"Even so, Tony, it will be enough of a mess for an ex-con just out of jail, carrying his concealed James Bond gun, to put him right back inside again, don't you think?"

Dodge stayed silent. He slowed the car as they reached the gates at Baldur's house.

"Drive through," Tree said.

Dodge rolled down the driver's side window, reached out to the digital pad built into the wall, hit some numbers, and when the gates started to open, moved the car forward.

"Swing around to the back," Tree said.

Dodge did as he was told. When the car stopped, Tree told him to get out. Tree eased himself out the back as Dodge opened his door. He stepped back an instant before Dodge lunged at him. Without thinking, Tree blindly pulled the trigger of the Walther PPK. The gun went off with an oddly muted pop. Dodge winced and grabbed his leg, sinking against the car.

"You shot me, man," he said in disbelief.

"You shouldn't have come at me like that," Tree said, trying to catch his breath.

"Man, I'm shot here," Dodge said. "You got to get me to a hospital."

"Sure thing, Tony. But first of all, you have to make a call."

"No way, man. You get me to a hospital."

"Listen, quit trying to negotiate your way out of this, or I swear I will shoot you again. Get on your phone. Make the call."

For the first time Tree saw something approximating fear cross Dodge's face. He was in a bad spot, and he knew it. He took out his Blackberry, holding it up as though it was the evidence of his co-operation.

"Call Fudd and Elmer," Tree said.

"Man, don't do this," Dodge whined.

"Call them. Say you're back at the house. There's an emergency. Get over here. Then hang up."

"Then you get me to a hospital, right? My leg's killing me."

"Call them."

He pressed something on the Blackberry, waited a moment, and then said: "Yeah, it's me. Get back to the house ASAP. Emergency."

Tree grabbed the Blackberry out of Dodge's hand, and dropped it into his pocket. Dodge winced and held his leg tighter. "Hurting bad, man."

Let's get you inside," Tree said.

Tree followed the limping, stumbling Dodge into the house. Indirect lighting cast the kitchen in amber light. Tree thought about how Freddie would kill for this kitchen.

Tree prodded Dodge through a series of corridors into a darkened sitting room the size of a hotel lobby. Dodge staggered against a suede sofa, dripping blood.

"You got to listen to me, man. I need a doctor bad. Okay? This is no fooling around. I'm bleeding all over the place."

"Tell me Tony, did Ferne and Slippery beg you to take them to a hospital?"

"I didn't have nothing to do with that."

"You didn't kill Brand Traven. You didn't kill Kendra. Now you had nothing to do with murdering Ferne and Slippery. But you know, Tony, since you got out of prison a lot of people have died."

"Those two clowns Baldur hired, that's their specialty. It ain't mine. Your lady friend should never have taken a baseball bat to them. They've been waiting to get her."

"If you didn't kill Brand Traven and Kendra, did those two?"

That got a wry smile out of Dodge. "Man, every time I start to think you might actually have a brain in your head, you remind me how stupid you are. If I was gonna kill someone, I sure as hell wouldn't use scissors to do it. Traven's old lady killed him, not because he wanted her out of the business, but because he wanted *in*. That's why he got me out of Coleman. He and Baldur wanted to take over the whole business; they didn't like the way it was being run. They needed someone familiar with this kind of operation. Traven knew I'd been involved in high-end situations in Detroit and New York and could give them the results they were looking for."

"What about Kendra?"

"I don't know," Dodge said. "The way I hear it, she was playing a lot of ends against the middle. Your guess is as good as mine."

"What about Baldur?"

"What about him?"

"Could he have done it?"

"I thought he was crazy about her, wanted her back after she ran out on him. Trouble with that dude, he's a whack job. Sometimes, he kills the things he loves. So who knows."

Dodge's Blackberry sounded in Tree's pocket. He pulled the device out and looked at the digital readout. It was Baldur. "Speak of the devil."

Tree handed Dodge the phone. He held it to his ear. "Yes?" He listened for a moment. "Okay."

Tree plucked the phone from Dodge's fingers. "What did he want?"

"He needs to be picked up."

Outside, Tree heard the sound of a car. Dodge made another pained face and said, "Now we're in for it. Those two morons are going to come in here, guns blazing."

"Take your jacket and tie off, Tony."

"What is this?"

"Take them off."

Dodge groaned and struggled out of his jacket and then undid his tie. Tree took them from him.

Tree heard a door opening. He pulled the jacket on. Not a great fit, but it would do. That's when Dodge all of a sudden found a strength Tree would not have thought he had left and charged him for a second time.

Tree fired wildly, missing Dodge who lost his balance and fell across a coffee table. Fudd appeared in the room and, thinking someone was shooting at him in the darkness, returned fire. Dodge, trying to get to his feet, screamed in pain as one of Fudd's bullets hit him and he pitched forward.

Tree dropped the Walther then turned and groped his way out of the living room into the twisting corridors leading to the front entrance.

Outside, the warm night was a pleasant contrast to the artificially arctic temperature inside the Baldur house.

Tree stumbled down the front steps expecting Fudd and Elmer to come crashing out of the house after him. He reached the car and opened the driver's door and found the chauffeur's cap, crown down on the passenger seat. He laid his Glock beside the cap and started the car.

He heard more gunshots inside the house.

44

Tree felt suddenly woozy as he drove the Lincoln away from Baldur's house. The adrenalin rush that accompanied kidnapping Tony Dodge and getting involved in a shootout had worn off. Everything began hurting again.

He glanced at himself in the rear view mirror. He looked terrible. His mouth was a bloody mess, not helped by the fact that two of his front teeth were missing. The side of his face throbbed and had begun to swell and turn purple. He adjusted the chauffeur's cap so that the peak was lower on his forehead, and he kept driving.

The return to the Ringling Museum grounds took only minutes. Security guards waved him through the main gate. The Lincoln's headlights captured departing guests flooding either side of the drive leading to the mansion. Were they leaving or escaping Jay and the Americans?

He pulled up to the side entrance. A beefy security guard rapped on the window and Tree rolled it down.

"Mr. Baldur's been waiting for you," the guard said.

"I'm here," Tree said.

"He ain't a happy man." The guard shook his head sympathetically. His face disappeared. A moment later, Baldur wheeled out the door, a stunning young woman hanging off either arm. The guard yanked open the rear passenger door so Baldur could guide his ladies inside. They giggled delightedly.

One of the women was blond with short hair. The other had long black hair, like a ribbon of silk in the shadowy interior. Both were very young. Too young, perhaps.

Baldur said, "Where have you been? Let's get out of here."

Tree started the car forward. The women giggled some more. Baldur exhaled loudly and said, "Was that a night? What did you think of Jay and the Americans? Weren't they great?"

"Who are they?" said a female voice. "I never heard them before."

"You never heard of Jay and the Americans?" Baldur sounded taken aback. "They are world famous. We were very lucky to get them."

Silence from the rear. Baldur said, "It was a great night." As if trying to convince himself.

"Awesome," one of the women said.

"There should have been more press," Baldur said. "Where was the *New York Times?* I didn't see anyone from the *Times.*"

More silence. Tree chanced a quick glance at the rear view mirror. Baldur was on his iPhone. "Hey, Sophie," he said. "Yeah, great. But what about *The Times? The New York Times.* Did their reporter attend? No? What about *U.S.A. Today?* I thought they were going to have someone."

He grew sullen. "Sophie, don't tell me what you can't do, okay? I don't want to hear that. I only want to hear what you can do. What I'm hearing is that no reporters from the national press were there. Well, that's what I'm hearing, so no, I'm not happy."

He must have turned off the phone. Tree heard him mutter, "I don't like this."

"Come on Aksel," one of the young women said. "You said you had stuff."

"Shut up," Baldur snapped. Then, his voice rose, "Hey, why so slow, driver? Come on. Speed it up."

Tree pressed his foot against the accelerator, and the Lincoln leapt smartly forward. In the back it grew quiet. Tree hazarded another peek at the rear view mirror. Baldur was wrapped around the blonde, her reward for not complaining about Jay and the Americans.

He sped along the road, approaching a marina on the right. He slowed and turned into the parking lot. He leapt out, pulling the Glock at the same time as he opened the passenger door.

"Get out," he ordered the startled occupants.

Baldur and his friends looked at Tree like he had landed from another planet. Baldur's face suddenly lit with recognition. "Callister? Are you out of your mind?"

Tree pointed the Glock into the car and repeated, "Get out."

The blonde with short hair squealed. Baldur looked irritated. "Quiet down," he told her. "Do as he says. Get out of the car."

The beauty with silky hair showed lots of leg as she slid from the vehicle. Baldur followed and then the blonde, reduced to sniffles. Tree kept the gun trained on Baldur.

"I want you to drive," Tree said.

Baldur smiled and said, "Get out of the car. Drive. Do this. Do that. All these orders, Callister. What? Just because you have a gun?"

"No," Tree said, "because tonight I've been handcuffed to two corpses, attacked by alligators, and I've already shot one guy. I don't see any reason in the world why I shouldn't shoot you."

That wiped the smile off Baldur's face. "I told them not to hurt you."

"Well, they weren't listening."

"What do you want, Callister?"

"Give your friends some money. I'm sure they've got cell phones. As soon as we're gone, they can call a cab. If I were you, I'd advise them not to call the police. This is going to be messy enough. I don't think you want the police involved, not yet, anyway."

"I don't have any money," Baldur said.

"You're rich," Tree said.

"I never carry cash." He looked at the women. "You have any money?"

They both shook their heads.

"This is unbelievable," Tree said.

"Why don't you let me drive them home, and you save your money?" Baldur said.

Tree fished into his pocket and came out with a couple of twenty dollar bills. He handed the cash to the silky beauty.

Baldur turned and spoke quietly to her. "Do as he says, okay? Don't call the police. Let me handle this."

"Aksel, for God's sake," the blonde said, "he's got a gun."

"It's America," Baldur said calmly. "Everyone's got a gun. Get a cab. Go home. I'll call you later."

He kissed the blonde's forehead. That started her crying again. He bussed the silky beauty's cheek—the Finnish Sidney Carton, sacrificing himself for the far, far better thing. Baldur pushed his heavy bulk behind the wheel of the Lincoln. Tree got in beside him.

"What do you want me to do?" Baldur said.

Tree suddenly realized he had no idea. "Just drive," he said.

45

Y ou look awful," Baldur said, keeping his eyes on the road.

"People have been trying to kill me," Tree said. "It makes for a lot of wear and tear."

"For what it's worth, you surprised me back there," Baldur said.

"Is that so?"

"The last thing I expected you to do."

"Yes, well I have this knack for doing the unexpected."

"So here we are, messy, as you say. How do we get out of it? You are angry, I can see that, and maybe I don't blame you. But anger isn't going to solve either of our problems. What will help, I suppose, is for you to achieve whatever it is you are seeking. So tell me, Tree Callister, what are you after?"

"A confession."

"I am not good at confessions. Ask the old priest where I grew up. Confession is a nice way of admitting guilt, and I dislike guilt. It gets in the way of what you have to do."

"Then just tell me why you killed Kendra."

Baldur kept his eyes fixed ahead while he sadly shook his head. "You are mistaken if you think I had anything to do with Kendra's death."

"You and Kendra and a belt. The two of you have done it before. I have the photos to prove it."

Baldur shot him a glance. "I loved Kendra," he said quietly. "I should not have been so stupid, but then love makes you stupid, doesn't it? That is my failing: falling in love with a loveless woman, not killing her."

"That's not what Kendra thought. You scared her and her husband badly enough that they ran away."

"Listen to me. I did not want to hurt her, no matter what she and her husband told you. I was the one protecting Kendra, trying to save her ass, save us all when it came down to it."

"From what?"

"Brand Traven's murder. I no sooner hear of it than Kendra comes crying into my arms saying she didn't know what happened, and what was she going to do now?"

"What are you saying? Kendra murdered Brand Traven?"

"She went to him about business, furious at the way he was attempting to interfere. There was some sort of confrontation, a pair of scissors ..."

"I don't believe it," was all Tree could think of to say.

"What? You don't think Kendra was capable of murder? If that's the case my friend, you didn't know her very well."

"But why didn't Elizabeth tell this to the police?"

"Elizabeth did not know Kendra went to see her husband. Kendra waited until she was out of town, arranging some business things."

"You mean procuring women for you."

"Not just for me. Many clients were interested in what Red Rose was offering. It's a very lucrative business that has saved not only Elizabeth's fortunes but mine as well. The shame is that Kendra's jealousy and greed destroyed it for all of us."

"Which brings me back to you killing her to get her out of the way."

"Such action, had I taken it, would have been carefully planned and meticulously executed by someone like Mr. Dodge. No, Kendra died as the result of a crime of passion."

"You're certainly capable of that."

"Perhaps," Baldur said. "But it was not me."

"Then who was it?"

"I think you know, Mr. Callister. You just don't want to admit it."

"Why don't you tell me."

"Your son, of course. Who had a better reason to kill her?"

Before Tree could answer him, something crashed into the Lincoln from behind.

Baldur lost control of the car and it veered off the road straight into a lamppost. A slow motion halo of glass sprayed through the interior. The passenger side air bag deployed, a big white pillow bursting to embrace Tree.

The world blurred and came to a stop. Tree felt as though he was floating in space. Perhaps he was dying, his soul departing his body. He did not want to think about where that soul might be headed.

Then the sound of hissing steam and settling metal reached him. He heard Baldur groan beside him. Instinctively, he reached for the latch, got the door open and fell out of the car onto the pavement.

He sat up, trying to clear his head. A green minivan lay crumpled against the rear of the Lincoln. The van's windshield folded out tent-like. He saw Fudd stagger through the steam rising from the destroyed van. He had lost his glasses. Blood streamed down his pear-shaped face. He had a gun in his hand. He began firing blindly at nothing in particular, as if shooting a gun would solve everything.

Other forms jumped into focus. The forms wore blue, and they too held guns. They returned fire. Fudd came to a stop, as though hearing something in the distance. Then he was flung backward, yanked hard by invisible wires.

The sound of more gunfire echoed eerily through the fog beginning to cover everything. Tree was tired. He lay back on the pavement. Not very comfortable, he thought.

But it would do for now.

46

Tree lay on a crimson desert. Buzzards circled lazily overhead, in no hurry to pick at his bones. Lifting his head, he saw a man moving toward him through the heat waves rising off the desert floor.

A cowboy from the look of him, tall and broad-shouldered, walking with a curious, rolling gait. A battered and stained white Stetson shaded his eyes. He carried a saddle in one hand, a Winchester rifle in the other. A mangy-looking dog followed at his booted heels.

When he spotted Tree, the cowboy came to a stop and lowered the saddle to the ground. The dog hunched and bared its teeth. The cowboy moved closer, and Tree could see that his face was rugged and lined, etched with the history of the American West.

"I need help," Tree managed to say.

The cowboy put the rifle to one side and knelt to Tree. The dog stopped snarling and stretched out on the ground not far away.

"I've got to get to my son, I've got to help him," Tree said.

"Right now, you're not going anywhere," the cowboy said in a gentle voice. "You're pretty badly hurt."

"I've got to help him," Tree repeated. "I can't let him down."

The cowboy sadly shook his head. "I'm afraid this is it, partner. You're going to die right here."

"No," Tree gurgled.

"Sorry friend, you don't have a lot of choice in the matter. This is your life unfolding before your eyes, but I'm the hero, not you. You're just a fella lost in the desert. A bit player in your own story, the character who dies so that I can go on and achieve the goals I've set out for myself."

"I don't want to die," Tree said. "I want to be the hero and save my son."

"Life will get you partner, it always does. Only in the movies do you live forever, and you ain't in the movies. You're in real life where there are no happy endings. That's why I made so many pictures. Three or four a year."

"Yes," said Tree. "I've always wondered about that. Why did you make so many?"

"Because there are no troubles on a movie set," he said. "When the camera stops rolling, that's when the trouble starts."

"But there are no cameras."

"That's why you're in life, and I'm in movies."

Tree began to tremble. Or was someone shaking him? He opened his eyes. Freddie bent over him. He thought she looked so lovely, even with that worried expression on her face. She said, "Tree, wake up. You had a bad dream."

"He got it wrong," Tree said.

"Who got it wrong?"

"John Wayne. He said there are no happy endings in life. But there are because here you are, and I'm alive, and everything is going to be all right."

Freddie gently kissed him. "What am I going to do with you?"

"Where am I?"

"Sarasota Memorial Hospital."

There were bandages around his torso. A gauze pad was taped to his forehead. His right hand had been dressed.

"How am I doing?" he asked Freddie.

"You tell me."

"I'm not sure. I can't feel anything."

"That's because they've got you nicely drugged. You've suffered broken ribs, lacerations to your face, and a badly sprained hand which must have happened when you fell out of the car."

"I didn't fall out. I made a strategic exit."

"The good news is that the doctors think you will live. However, they have asked me to point out something that you may not be aware of."

"What's that?"

"You're too old for this."

"The doctors don't know what they're talking about."

"Of course not," Freddie said. "How could they?" She perched on the edge of the bed, smiling down at him. "There is one other thing."

"What is it?"

"You are missing two front teeth."

"That's because someone kicked them out."

"Yes," Freddie said. "I thought it might be something like that."

"I'm afraid you've got a toothless husband," he said.

"As long as I've got a husband," she said.

He couldn't be certain, but he thought he saw a tear roll down her cheek.

47

It took some time to unravel the details of what had happened.

The Sarasota police found the body of Tony Dodge after they had been called to the home of the late Aksel Baldur by neighbors hearing gunshots.

Dodge was Anthony Thomas Dodge from Detroit. He had recently been released from Coleman Prison where he had served ten years for manslaughter. The Detroit police said he had worked for the city's Tocco and Zerrilli crime families. He had gone to prison convicted of manslaughter after an FBI informant was beaten to death.

From what police could piece together, there had been a falling out between Dodge and two other Baldur security men, Emile Nappi and Carl Whitman. Tree knew them better as Fudd and Elmer. Nappi, aka Fudd, had a long criminal record that included extortion, aggravated assault and car theft. Whitman, bear-like Elmer, had been tried for two murders that ended with hung juries.

Both men had been wounded in the course of the shootout that killed Dodge. Despite their wounds, and for reasons still unclear to investigators, the two gunmen had gone after their employer.

A single gunshot to the head had killed Aksel Baldur. The shot had been fired by Nappi as he stumbled from the minivan after it crashed into Baldur's Lincoln. Whitman was pried out of the crushed remains and declared dead on arrival at hospital.

The police were anxious to know what Tree Callister, badly beaten with two missing front teeth, was doing in a car with Aksel Baldur.

Tree explained that he had come to Sarasota to question Aksel Baldur after finding explicit photos showing Baldur and Kendra having sex.

Tree said he met Baldur at the Ringling mansion after the unveiling of Aksel's spring collection (the reviews in the fashion press had not been good). They were driving away when their Lincoln was rammed by the minivan driven by Fudd and Elmer.

Privately, trying to rationalize what had happened, Tree speculated that since he had witnessed the shootout with Dodge, the two thugs were coming after him and not Baldur. Crashing into the Lincoln was probably a misguided attempt on their part to rescue Baldur. Tree could not think of a reason why he should tell the police any of this.

Over the objections of lawyer Edith Goldman, Tree received a hospital visit from Sanibel Detective Owen Markfield. Before he died, Tree said, Aksel Baldur told him that Kendra Callister confessed to murdering Brand Traven after the two had fought over their high-end sex business.

Convenient, Markfield observed, that Baldur had fingered a dead woman just before he died. However, the police had matched Kendra's DNA with traces found at the Traven house. While there were other possible explanations for the presence of her DNA, the prosecutors no longer believed they had enough evidence to convict Elizabeth Traven, and she was released.

There was talk of charging her with soliciting and procurement in connection with the sex trafficking ring, although Elizabeth vehemently denied any involvement.

Left open was the question of who killed Kendra Callister.

Markfield still favored Tree for the crime. But now there were the photos of Aksel with a belt wrapped around Kendra's throat, and the late clothing designer became the most likely suspect. There was, Tree was relieved to note, no talk of his son Chris being charged.

Kendra's parents, Bill and Anita Dean, arrived on the island. After they collected their daughter's body, they took her back to Marshall, Missouri where Kendra had grown up and attended Missouri Valley College. Bill Dean was manager of the local Walmart. Anita taught business at the college. Freddie tried to reach out to them, but they refused to even take her phone call.

48

Five days after he was admitted to hospital, Tree was released. Freddie helped him to her car.

"I'm still mad at you," she said.

"Even though your battered knight errant is coming home?"

"The battered knight errant who doesn't tell me everything."

"That's not true." Not sure he was telling her the truth.

"I don't like it when you keep things from me, Tree. I can handle just about anything in connection with this private detective business, including you losing two front teeth, but I can't handle us not being truthful with one another."

"Okay, here's something I haven't told you: I don't think Baldur killed Kendra."

"What about those photos?"

"I'm not saying they didn't do kinky things. But when I spoke to him in the car just before he died, he was pretty convincing that he didn't kill her."

"That leaves Chris."

"Baldur thought he did it."

"What do you think?"

"I think maybe that's why I'm not telling you every-thing."

When they arrived back at Andy Rosse Lane, the front door opened as Freddie helped Tree out of the Mercedes. Chris, pale and grim, stepped into view.

He said, "I drove up to see you, but you were kind of out of it."

"It's all right, Chris," Tree said.

"I just want you to know that, Dad. I don't want you to think I wasn't there."

"Chris, it's okay. It doesn't make any difference."

"Yes, it does," Chris said.

They stood looking at each other and then, somehow, they were in each other's arms. Tree held onto his son for dear life, and Chris kept repeating that he was sorry.

They sat together on the terrace beside the pool, Fred-die diplomatically fading away inside to prepare something to eat.

Chris said, "You shouldn't have done it, Dad. You shouldn't have put yourself out there for me."

"Right now, all the evidence is pointing to Aksel Bal-dur, so I think we're going to be okay."

"But you don't believe he did it."

"I'm not saying that."

"But you know what no one else knows, don't you, Dad? You know that when you came into the house, there I was sitting downstairs, and there she was upstairs, dead. You're trying to protect me, I know, and you've done a pretty good job of it, but you keep thinking it must be Chris, it has to be my son. That's the only logical explana-tion."

Tree didn't say anything.

Chris's gaze remained steady, as steady as Tree had seen it for a long time. "I know how it probably looks, and I know I got myself into some pretty questionable things, okay? And the night you found me, I didn't tell you the whole truth."

Tree felt his stomach drop. "What didn't you tell me?"

"I tied the belt around her neck."

"You what?"

"It was a thing we did. For sex. She liked it. I liked it too, I suppose."

"You told me Kendra was dead when you found her."

"That wasn't true," Chris said. "I left for a half hour or so. After we finished making love, she said she was having trouble sleeping, she needed sleeping pills. Nothing too strong. Over-the-counter stuff. I drove to the drug store on the island, the one just off Periwinkle on Library Way, got something for her and then arrived back maybe three quarters of an hour later. That's when I found her dead in the bedroom. I didn't know what to do. I knew how it looked. I went downstairs, trying to think. That's when you showed up."

Tree said, "The police are probably not going to believe you."

"I know that. But it's the truth. It's what I want to tell the police."

Freddie called them for dinner. Maybe Chris was right. Maybe he should talk to the police and get it over with, and put a stop to the lies.

They went inside to Freddie and a lovely chicken dish for Chris—tomato soup for toothless Tree. How the conversation had changed, Tree reflected. Not long ago it was school and marks and how Chris's mother was getting along; strained neutral topics to be sure, but the stuff of life. Now it was who might or might not be a killer. However, there remained one constant after a lifetime of conversations with his son: nothing was resolved.

The telephone rang. Freddie rose to get it. She came back holding out the portable receiver. "You better take this."

The voice on the line said, "Hello, Mr. Callister, this is Elizabeth Traven speaking."

"Hello, Mrs. Traven."

"I've been released from jail."

"So I've heard."

"I thought I'd phone and see how you're doing."

"I'm coming along," Tree said.

"You've been through a rough time."

"What is it, Mrs. Traven? Why have you called?"

"I was hoping we might get together," she said.

"Tonight?"

"Depending on how you're feeling, of course."

"I'm not feeling like seeing you tonight."

"Why don't we say about eight o'clock."

The line went dead.

49

This time he did not linger outside the house on Captiva Drive. This time Freddie drove him straight through the open gates.

Tree shivered, the way he would in a horror movie approaching the haunted house. A multitude of unwelcome revelations and a murder had all played out here. Tree steeled himself as Freddie came to a stop in front of the steps leading to the entrance.

"Are you all right?"

"I don't want to do this."

"Then don't, my love."

"Well, I hate to say—"

"What? A man's got to do what a man's got to do?"

"I was thinking along simpler lines: I have to do this."

Freddie rolled her eyes. "You and Rex watch too many John Wayne movies. Do you want me to come in with you?"

"Yes, but if it's all right, I think you'd better wait here."

She kissed his mouth. "Come back in half an hour. If you don't, I'm calling the police."

He got out of the car and went up the steps. As always, the stone Great Danes flanking the staircase watched him with impassive disdain. As he approached the entrance, the front door opened and T. Emmett Hawkins materialized. Tonight he wore a red bow tie with white polka-dots.

"Good evening, Mr. Callister. Thanks for coming over at such short notice."

"Where is she?"

"Inside. Waiting."

Tree felt as if he was floating through the interior. Nothing was real here. Everything was shadows and lies, the washing sea a sound effect in the distance. He drifted behind Hawkins into the living room. The floor-to-ceiling windows presented the final moments of the daily spectacle that was the sun dying. The sofa on which Brand Traven died had been removed. The space it occupied remained empty, a poignant reminder in case anyone tried to forget what happened in this room.

Hawkins stepped away to reveal Elizabeth Traven in an armchair near the window. She wore a short tan skirt that showed off the legs Tree had tried so hard not to admire. The sun's final rays set her beauty on fire.

She looked up at him and said, "What happened to your front teeth?"

"Everyone asks me that," Tree said.

"You don't look good, Mr. Callister. You had better sit down."

"That's all right," Tree said. "I'd rather stand."

Elizabeth reached over and picked up a thick envelope from an end table. She tossed it to Tree. He fumbled the catch; the envelope dropped to the floor. Hawkins pointed a sausage-like finger.

"There is one hundred and fifty thousand dollars in there."

Tree addressed Elizabeth. "That's too much."

"Given the cost of a good dentist these days, I don't think so. It's yours. Pick it up."

Tree did not touch the envelope. Elizabeth's smile disappeared. "What's the matter?"

"You used me," he said.

"I hired you to watch my husband because I thought he was going to kill me. This Tony Dodge character was the evidence he was planning to do precisely that."

"And you didn't kill Brand Traven?"

"No, Mr. Callister, I didn't. Thanks to your efforts, we now know that Kendra committed the crime."

"What about the sex trafficking?" Tree said.

"You mean the business of providing attractive, willing young women for rich stupid men? If that's a crime, it's at the very bottom of a formidable list."

She waved her hand in the way she could when she wanted to be dismissive. "Besides, there is nothing to these allegations as far as I'm concerned." She arose from her chair, majestic and beautiful in the fading light, her sensuality undiminished by a few weeks in jail.

"Right now, I'd like nothing better than to put all this behind me, Tree. There is nothing to be gained for anyone in continuing these accusations and counter-accusations. You can help me put a stop to all this once and for all so we all can get back to our normal lives."

"I don't see how I can help you, Mrs. Traven."

"The district attorney's office continues to make threatening noises about this prostitution thing. It's an irritant, really, but one that has to be addressed."

Tree waited. Hawkins cleared his throat. Elizabeth suddenly smiled and stepped forward and ran a soft hand across his cheek. "You look so stern and tense, Tree. It's all right."

"What is it, Mrs. Traven?"

She took her hand away. "It is Mr. Hawkins' under-standing that the police intend to charge your son with his wife's murder. Is that correct, Mr. Hawkins?"

Hawkins stepped forward and said, "I have it on good authority they will reduce the murder charge to manslaughter if Chris agrees to testify against Mrs. Traven in connection with these prostitution allegations."

"Chris didn't kill his wife," Tree said.

"That's unlikely to stop the police," Elizabeth said.

"What are you getting at?" Tree demanded.

"There's a check in that envelope for one hundred and fifty thousand dollars. That's for you. There is another one hundred and fifty thousand if Chris agrees not to testify against me. Also in the envelope is the information I think you will need in order to identify the real killer."

Hawkins stooped and scooped the envelope off the floor. He straightened, red faced, and held it out to Tree. "Everything you need is in here," he said.

"What if you're lying to me yet again?" Tree said to Elizabeth.

"Then Chris will be arrested for murder, and I will be charged with running a prostitution ring," Elizabeth said, "and we will both go to jail—you, too, maybe."

Hawkins said, "What's it going to be, Mr. Callister? Do we have an agreement or not?"

"Tree," he heard Elizabeth Traven say. "What's the matter? Why don't you say something?"

He stared at the envelope.

50

It took Freddie and Tree less than an hour to reach Naples.

A single light burned inside the house on Gulf Shore Boulevard. They got out of the Mercedes and went to the entrance. Freddie rang the doorbell. No movement came from the interior. Freddie rang again and when nothing happened, Tree turned the latch and the door swung open. They traded glances. Freddie pushed the door open further and called, "Ray? Ray are you here? It's Freddie."

No answer. She entered the house, Tree following.

They found the Ray Man sitting in an armchair facing the ocean. One of the upsides of death along the West Coast of Florida, Tree thought. You got a lot of sea views.

Ray wasn't looking at the sea tonight. His head was thrown back so that he stared at the ceiling, the result of having placed a silver-plated revolver in his mouth and then pulling the trigger. The gun lay on the hardwood floor, not far from the chair.

The gunshot had blown the back of his skull over the headrest, bits and pieces flying across the room, splattering the wall. A pool of coagulated blood surrounded the chair. The Ray Man had been dead for a while.

When she saw him, Freddie gasped and put her fist against her mouth and began to tremble. Tree held her, turning her away. "Oh, God," Freddie said, and then repeated it several times.

Tree led her outside. The moon was nearly full. The gentle sound of the Gulf of Mexico against the shore was in the distance. A breeze only added to the beauty of a Florida night. You should not be blowing your brains out on a night like this.

Tree pulled out the envelope Elizabeth Traven had given him. He showed Freddie the typewritten pages. "It's a list of the Red Rose clientele. Ray is on it. I guess that's how he met Kendra."

"So he did know her."

"For close to a year. It looks like he went up to Chicago to visit her."

Freddie said, "What are you thinking?"

"That's why Kendra wanted to come here. Not because we were here, but because Ray was. She thought he would help her when Baldur came looking for her. And she was right, to a point."

"The question is, how did you find out about the two of them?"

"By accident. I was following Brand Traven and I ended up at the Lani Kai Resort in Fort Myers Beach just as they came out together."

"And you didn't tell me."

"I wasn't quite sure what to make of it at the time, and I didn't want to upset you unnecessarily."

"Don't worry about upsetting me, I'm a big girl," she said. "I repeat: I don't like it when you keep things from me—no matter how bad they are."

"I know you don't."

"But you hide more and more."

"I try not to."

"Well, try harder. I suppose that explains why you asked me about Ray's place in Naples."

Tree nodded. "When Aksel's thugs came looking for Kendra, he arranged for Chris and her to hide out here."

"But Ray being Ray, he wanted Kendra all to himself, so he moved her to the house on Woodring Road. Have I got that right?"

"I think so."

Freddie went on: "Maybe when he finally had her alone, maybe that's when it became apparent that Kendra was not going to be his true and everlasting love; she was not about to be any man's true love."

"Kendra used men. She wasn't crazy enough to fall in love with them."

"Ray wouldn't like that at all."

"According to Chris, Kendra phoned him. He went around to the house on Woodring Road. They ended up making love. That's when they used the belt."

Freddie arched her eyebrows. "A belt? What did they do with a belt?"

"Things we're not about to try at this stage in our lives," Tree said.

"Then Ray came to the house, is that how it happened?"

Tree nodded. "He was supposed to be at the Kiwanis dinner that night, but he never showed up."

"He would have seen Chris's car in the drive," Freddie said. "He must have slipped inside and overheard them making love. It would have made his blood boil."

"Then Chris left to go to the pharmacy for Kendra," Tree said. "Ray went upstairs, found her still in bed and used the belt to strangle her." He paused. "Of course this is all wild speculation."

"Except Ray is inside, dead," Freddie said.

Tree looked at her hard. She shrugged uneasily.

"I don't know. Does any of this make sense? I guess there isn't a suicide note."

"Not unless we missed it."

"Ray would never write something like that. It would be too hard for him to admit he could be so weak. Better he just shoots himself and leaves us all wondering: could Ray kill? I don't know the answer. I suspect I never will. Do we really believe anyone we know is capable of murder? I don't believe we do. But people end up killing each other all the time, don't they? So what are we to think? What are we supposed to think?"

"It's okay," he said.

"No, no, it's not. How did we get here, Tree? How did we get so far into darkness? How did we stumble into this world of corpses and people doing bad things? How did that happen?"

Tears streamed down her cheeks. Tree held her for a while. He didn't know what to say. He knew how they got here, and so did she. It was him; he was responsible for this. But having arrived in this dark place, he could not find the way out. He was trapped here.

Tree let go of her. He fished his cell phone out of his pocket and called 911.

51

"Last night I saw *The Searchers* for the first time in years," Rex Baxter said. "It really is John Wayne's greatest performance. No other star of that time came close to what he achieved, not Brando or Clift, no one played a character approaching the complexity of Ethan Edwards in that movie.

"And Tree is absolutely right," Rex went on. "*The Searchers* is as much a rumination on life and death as it is a western about the price of hatred and the cost of revenge. At the beginning, a door opens into the light, and at the end John Ford closes that door again, and we are alone in darkness. That's what it's about, isn't it? Infinite darkness interrupted briefly by light, all of us alone at the end. When it was over, I wept."

"Jeez, Rex," Todd Jackson said.

"I wept for us all, for the futility of life and the certainty of death, the knowledge as we get older that the door closes and we are alone in darkness, and there is nothing we can do about it."

"I've never heard you talk like this," Todd said.

"Well, there you go," Rex said. "Maybe it was the movie, or maybe it's just one of those nights."

Everyone had retreated to the Lighthouse after the services for Ray Dayton. Vera, Ray's widow, had decided not to attend, understandable under the circumstances. Besides, she had never liked Ray at the Lighthouse on Fun Fridays. She did not like what a few drinks did to him. No one did.

The previous day the police had released details of Kendra's autopsy. Two different types of semen had been found in her vagina. One of the types belonged to her husband, Chris.

The other was matched to the late Ray Dayton.

Nobody talked about any of it.

Finally, Todd Jackson ventured that he liked Ray; despite everything, he couldn't help but like the guy. After all, he had served his country in Vietnam. Someone pointed out that he hadn't actually served in Nam. He'd been a supply sergeant in the Philippines.

"Who cares?" Todd. "The fact is the guy put himself on the line for his country. How many of us can say that?"

Freddie, who had come to Sanibel Island because Ray hired her, said nothing. She didn't cry in front of everyone; that was not her style. But she stayed close to Tree, clasping his arm.

"A long time ago, I interviewed John Wayne's daughter," Tree said. "She told me that when her father died of cancer at the age of seventy-two, after more than two hundred movies, after all the people he had worked with over fifty-odd years in the business, the legends formed, awards won, none of it mattered. At the end, there wasn't a screen legend anywhere to be seen, simply an old man dying of cancer, surrounded by his family. That image has stuck with me ever since. John Wayne dying, his family around him."

Silence. Someone cleared his throat.

"I didn't like Ray, but I feel sorry for him," Tree continued. "He ended up alienating everyone, a lonely man desperately looking for love, willing to kill because he couldn't get it. He should have been like John Wayne. He should have had family with him. Someone should have been holding his hand as he left. This shouldn't have happened."

Freddie gripped his arm tighter. Nobody said anything.

———

Nearing sunset, Freddie and Tree turned off onto one of the manmade islands supporting the three bridges of the Sanibel Causeway. A few vehicles were parked facing the beach. A lone windsurfer sliced the shallows just off shore. A couple had set up lawn chairs in front of their SUV and sat drinking beer, awaiting the end of the day.

Freddie wrapped her arm around Tree and helped him down to the water's edge. The failing sun cast Freddie in a golden halo. The rising breeze turned her into a wind-blown siren of the sea—at least in Tree's eyes. He thought he had never loved her so much as he did at this moment.

"When I was in the Myakka State Park," he said, "they handcuffed me to the bodies of Ferne Clowers and Bailey Street, although they call Bailey, 'Slippery.'"

She looked at him closely. "Slippery Street?"

Tree moved his head up and down in acknowledgment. "In order to get free and not become dinner for a couple of alligators, I used Slippery's straight razor and cut their hands off."

He marveled at how lovely she looked even with her eyes widened in astonishment.

"Slippery carried a straight razor around?"

"That's the kind of guy Slippery was."

"I see." The evening shadows heightened Freddie's astonished look.

"Well," he said. "You don't want me holding things back from you."

"No," she said.

"So I thought I had better tell you."

"My God, Tree," she said. "I married an unemployed Chicago newspaperman who once drank too much."

"I don't know what happened to that guy," Tree said.

She said, "What are you going to do about Chris?"

"What can I do?" Tree said. "He's my son. I have to stand by him."

The sun was disappearing below the horizon in a bright yellow explosion. The war of the worlds was being fought out there somewhere beyond the horizon.

"I just want you to know," Freddie said.

"What?"

"That I'm with you in this. Whatever it takes."

"Even though I'm missing two front teeth?"

"Even though," she said softly.

"I love you," he said.

"And we won't die alone, Tree. We will die with each other. Whatever we have to go through, we do it together. We share the pain. That's what it's all about, after all. The pain as well as the happiness. Deal?"

"Deal," he said.

The sun turned crimson an instant before the sea swallowed it, and the day was gone.

Tree kissed Freddie and she kissed him back, and then they turned and headed away from the shore toward the car.

Together.

Acknowledgements

Like Tree Callister, my paper in 1975 sent me down to Newport Beach, California, to interview John Wayne at his home. And just like Tree, Wayne promptly pumped me full of tequila, a drink I had never had before and have never had since.

I suffered accordingly the following day.

He was sixty-eight when I met him and had just starred in a now-forgotten police thriller called *Brannigan*. Watching him move gracefully and comfortably through his memorabilia-filled living room, I reached the same conclusion Tree does: it was hard to imagine the iconic western hero in a cowboy hat, a six-gun strapped to his waist, riding a horse.

But otherwise, he was everything you might imagine: blustery, outrageous, bigger-than-life, and vastly entertaining. Out on the patio overlooking the harbor and an old wood-frame pavilion across the way, he did tell the story that's in the book about how he used to go dancing there as a kid, laughing that these days he and the pavilion were all that was lit up at night.

It's funny how certain images keep reasserting themselves as you are writing a book. As I toiled away on *The Sanibel Sunset Detective Returns,* I kept seeing that moment on the patio, the Duke, as everyone called him, wearing a blue blazer, not as tall as I imagined, and looking a bit like someone had pumped him full of air. I understood even way back then that I was meeting one of the most iconic figures in American movies, and that the moment was fleeting, and I had better mark it carefully.

As I stood there listening to him hold court, it was not difficult to see the history of talking movies right there in front of me. He had started out as gofer on silent films, graduated to the talkies and become the biggest star the movies ever produced. No other star made as many films or lasted as long (over fifty years) or remained so popular. No one was quite like him before he came along, and certainly there has been no one like him since. As Rex Baxter points out in the book, his kind of rugged masculine individuality has disappeared from the screen.

I found his presence curiously comforting as I wrote the book, recalling that encounter, from time to time replaying his old movies (particularly *The Searchers*), marveling again at how good he could be on the screen when he was working with a John Ford or a Howard Hawks. Is it too late to thank him for that constant memory of a pleasant evening long ago in Newport Beach? I think not. Nor is it too late to again thank George Anthony who, as the *Toronto Sun's* entertainment editor, took pity on a young reporter and John Wayne admirer and assigned him to the story. George and I have remained friends ever since.

A lot of people made this book possible, beginning with my brother Ric, who in addition to being the world's best brother, not to mention the president of the Sanibel-Captiva Chamber of Commerce, has become a partner in these Tree Callister adventures, a combination of publisher, marketing guru, and reliable island guide (although any mistakes in the book are mine, not his). I say this every time we do a book and it just becomes truer— I could not do any of it without his enthusiasm and support. What a bro!

And further words of heartfelt thanks to my sister-in-law Alicia, who patiently puts up with me, and provides great lines of dialogue which I enthusiastically steal.

I have met a large number of welcoming, wonderful people on Sanibel and Captiva islands who have been immeasurably helpful in making *The Sanibel Sunset Detective* a success. The chamber's Bridgit Stone-Budd not only did the brilliantly-executed, eye-catching covers for both novels, but also worked overtime to be present at book signings and generally help promote the book.

Richard Johnson at Bailey's allowed me into his store countless times; Hollie Schmid at the Sanibel Island Bookshop made me a bestselling author on the island. Thanks also to Scott and Candy Thompson, Paul and Susan Reynolds at PocoLoco, Chris Clark of Paradies Shops at the Fort Myers airport, John Tonsager at Jerry's Foods, Joanne Nappi at The Sporty Seahorse Shop, Duane Shaffer at the Sanibel Public Library, Susie Holly at MacIntosh Books and Paper, Josh Stewart at Adventures in Paradise, Barb Harrington at Royal Shell Vacations, and everyone at the Lighthouse Restaurant. Special thanks to Colleen and Earl Quenzel, my best customers. Back in Canada, the Milton Chamber of Commerce let me on the street and Sarah Moore allowed me into her bookstore. My neighbor and pal, Kim Hunter, got me to Florida and entertained along the way.

I'm fortunate to work with an incredible creative team that has no problem holding my feet to the fire and making me a better writer. My wife, Kathy Lenhoff, was, as always, first out of the gate to read the book and make helpful comments. My son, Joel Ruddy, was an early enthusiast for the latest Tree Callister adventure.

Old friend Ray Bennett, the *Hollywood Reporter's* London theater critic, read the manuscript while visiting in Toronto and made great suggestions. Lexie Lenhoff, with whom I have worked on every book I've written since 1990, once again saved me a hundred times over with her line editing, as did my daughter, Erin Ruddy, editor of *What's Up, Canada's Family Magazine.*

I am particularly indebted to another old journalism friend, Bob Burt, who really went to work on the book, and not only uncovered mistakes but identified plot inconsistencies, and generally contributed insights and suggestions that made me remember what a truly great editor he is. Thank you, Robert!

Finally, I must thank award-winning author and former journalist David Kendall, "the closer," who came in at the end of the process to make dozens of small, precise suggestions that resulted in a better book.

In the midst of everything this past year, my dear friend Brian Vallée died of cancer. Not only were we best pals for over forty years, but Brian, in addition to being an award-winning journalist, broadcaster, and bestselling author, was also the publisher of West-End Books. All of us who knew and loved him, including his long-time partner, Nancy Rahtz, were left in shock by the suddenness of his death. As I sit here writing these words, I still can't believe he is gone.

But that's part of the whole set-up, isn't it? Life and death, the door opening to let in the light for a brief period and then the door closing again into darkness. No one could have known it that night, of course, but less than four years later, John Wayne would be gone. He would make only one more movie, the classic *The Shootist*. He gave few intimations of mortality that night, merrily holding forth with a glass of tequila in his hand. But the next day, suffering, he admitted, a monstrous hangover, he was more reflective.

"Now I have yachting friends and tennis friends," he said of his life in Newport Beach. "I try not to get caught up in a little group where—where it really hurts to lose someone. When (silent western star) Harry Carey died, that was a great loss. I was a younger man then, and it was a shock to find that people die."

"But now we know they do."

We know all too well. Hail and farewell, John Wayne, and you too, Vallée B. I could not have made it through without the two of you.

Coming Soon

A New Tree Callister Adventure

Another Sanibel Sunset Detective

Read Ron's blog at
Ronbase.wordpress.com
e-mail Ron at
ronbase@ronbase.com
Check out The Sanibel Sunset Detective Website
ronbase@ronbase.com

be obtained at www.ICGtesting.com

B/1/P

9 780973 695557